Write It Right:

Exercises to Unlock the Writer in Everyone

* * *

Workbook #3

Units 5, 6: Plot, Dialogue

By
Susan Tuttle

Susan Tuttle

Write It Right:
Exercises to Unlock the Writer In Everyone
Unit 5: Plot
Unit 6: Dialogue

Susan's website and blog: www.SusanTuttleWrites.com
Email Susan at: aim2write@yahoo.com
Follow Susan on Twitter: @stuttleauthor, Facebook and LinkedIn

Cover design by: Aaron Kondziela (www.aaronkondziela.com)

A WriterWithin Publication

ISBN-10: 19141465048
ISBN-13: 978-1-941465-04-2

Write It Right:

Exercises to Unlock the Writer in Everyone

Workbook #3:

Plot, Dialogue

Dedication

The first unit contained herein, *Plot*, is dedicated to my son, Aaron Kondziela. A true 21st Century Renaissance Man, he is my computer guru and a wonderful graphic artist who designs my book covers. He's also a composer, cinematographer, lighting technician, special effects artist, photographer and philosopher. Pretty much anything he sets his mind on, he can do.

When he was young, I used to read him chapters of my books as bedtime stories. He gave me the best writing advice I've ever received. Whenever I would indulge in my love of exposition (to be honest, it's more like an obsession), he would sigh and say, "Too much character development, Mom. Get back to the story." Now when I find myself straying too far a distance from my plots, I hear his sigh in my head and I head out of the narrative jungle, back to the story. So, Aaron, this one's for you.

Dialogue, the second unit in this second Workbook, and the sixth in the *Write It Right* series, is dedicated to my mother, Shirley Young Tuttle. I still remember her when I was young. She would finish the breakfast dishes, sit down with a cup of coffee and a cigarette (back before we knew how bad they are for you) and chat on the phone with one of her four sisters. As I played in the background, I had to imagine the "hidden" end of the conversation, extrapolating from the things my mother said. It was the world's best preparation for creating dialogue a writer ever had. Wish you were still here to see these *Write It Right* volumes, Mom.

Contents

Before You Begin

SUCCESSFUL STORYTELLING LIES IN being able to tell the story you need to tell in the way readers need to hear it. When we do that, we create stories that readers cannot put down. There are many steps along the way. The first three, Character, Setting and Story, are contained in Workbook #1. The next most important element, Point of View, is presented in Workbook #2. This volume contains the next two most important skills: *Plot* and *Dialogue*.

Unlike other books on writing, this volume is designed as a workbook to help you hone your writing skills and find your unique voice. Within these pages, you will find **16 exercises** designed **for writers of all levels** that will show you how to craft enthralling tales readers will clamor for. You will discover strategies to developing unique stories that enthrall readers, and take them to places they've never before been. And you'll learn the secrets of crafting realistic dialogue that hooks readers, imparts information and moves your stories along, while your characters come alive for your readers.

In the few pages that follow is all the front matter that most people simply skip. If you haven't started with Workbook #1, please read what follows, especially the *Foreword* and *The Value of Timed Writing*. They contain invaluable information you will need to get the most out of these lessons and exercises. And even if you have read it already, please at least skim *The Value of Timed Writing*, to reacquaint yourself with the "rules" of each lesson.

And of course, don't skip the book list. They are all treasures for your writing library.

Foreword

WRITING IS MY LIFE. I have a thousand stories knocking on the inside of my head, seeking the freedom of paper. I also love to learn, especially about writing and ways to improve my range and skills. But I'm not very disciplined when it comes to how-to books. If it's not a mystery or suspense novel, I lose interest quickly, even if the subject matter is fascinating.

I found that, for me, the best way to learn something is to teach it to someone else. So, three-plus years ago, I decided to start a group where I could teach what I wanted to learn about writing techniques. If nothing else, it would force me to read those "how to write" books I've been collecting.

I formed the "*What If?* Writing Group" through SLO NightWriters on the Central Coast of California. I began with a group of six writers of various writing skills and genres. We met once a week for two hours to explore in depth a specific aspect of fiction writing. I worried at first that, given the weekly commitment, the group would gradually peter out. But not only did they keep showing up, they started arranging appointments and planning trips around the lessons so they wouldn't miss any!

As the year began winding down, I was sure this group would go on its literary way, and I wondered how to attract a new group of students. But when the year was up only one person left the group, due to health problems. Everyone else wanted to repeat the course. We picked up three new members and started again from the beginning, not sure if the original six students would get anything much from the repetition. To the contrary, we discovered the exercises worked just as well as the first time around—and in some instances, even better. It seems that, no matter where you are in your writing journey, or how many times you do these exercises, they continue to work. Every time.

These writers are now getting published on a regular basis, and winning awards in writing contests. In fact, three of us won first place awards in different categories at the Central Coast Writers Conference in September of 2011. One even came home with three prizes in the competition! For me, this was proof positive that the **Write It Right** exercises had a hand in unlocking the talent of every member of the group. That's why I added an afternoon class and 8 more students.

The writing successes of both of the *"What If? Writing Group"* made me wish I could reach more writers with the materials we'd used. But even if I taught classes all day, every day, I could reach only a limited number of writers—and all of them local. I wanted more than that. I wanted to reach all writers, everywhere.

To that end, I decided to collect all the lessons into a series of 6 little instruction workbooks (12 units in all), a full program called ***Write It Right: Exercises to Unlock the Writer in Everyone***. This workbook is the third Workbook of the series. The first two Workbooks (Character, Setting, Story and POV) are available in print and digital format from Amazon.com.

Introduction to Workbook #3

WITHOUT A VIABLE PLOT, there's no point in creating compelling characters, or crafting fascinating settings. Or even searching for great story ideas. **Plot is what changes an anecdote into a story**. It's the motivating factor that makes the characters act and react. It's the framework on which all the words you write are hung, all working toward a single goal: growth, change and a satisfying conclusion. Yet so many writers struggle with both finding a plot and staying true to it. I've often heard writers say, "I've got some great characters but I don't quite know what to do with them. I can't think of a plot." And yet, plots are all around us. If we know how and where to look, we will never run out of plots.

Dialogue can be one of the most frustrating elements of good fiction, creative nonfiction and memoir. **All** dialogue **must** impart information, develop character and move the plot along, all while sounding just like normal speech. If it doesn't, at best it will pull readers out of the story. At worst, it will leave them laughing and determined not to read anything else written by you.

That is where this Workbook comes in. The exercises that follow will give you the strategies you need to understand plot and how it works in the telling of a story, and help you develop the skill you need to discover more plots than you can possibly write. The eight lessons on dialogue will help you understand the full purpose of dialogue so you can write dialogue that will entrance and entice readers. Dialogue that will truly make your characters come alive.

It won't happen overnight. It takes practice. But the more you work with Plot and Dialogue, the better you will become at recognizing even the most subtle deviations in your narrative.

It doesn't matter what level you are: beginner, intermediate or advanced. These exercises cross those boundaries and address where you are now in your writing career—and get you to where you want to be.

These are not time-intensive sessions. You only need to **dedicate approximately 30-45 minutes** to most of the sixteen activities (a few may take longer). Feel free to move at your own pace—one or two exercises a week or a month—but if you choose a fast-track pace, do give yourself enough time assimilate each lesson. It's best to have a couple of days between each exercise. (The *"What If? Writing Group,"* which has used these lessons for over three years as of this writing, does one or two exercises per session, with a week between sessions.)

All you need is a timer and something to write with—pen and paper or computer and keyboard, whichever is most comfortable for you. For maximum results, you might want to pick up a copy of some of the books I've used to formulate these lessons, and which I will reference throughout the course. It's not necessary, though it does make understanding some of the concepts easier.

You can use this volume as a workbook, filling in the pages (though you will need extra paper to finish most of the exercises) as you work through the lessons. But it is best to use separate sheets of paper, or work digitally in a word processing program, so that when you return to the lessons as you feel the need you won't be distracted by previous answers to the lesson questions.

Always remember, this is an ongoing process. Writing is a dynamic art and life is a journey through which you are always growing and learning. Over time your writing will expand and deepen to reflect these life experiences. When you finish this volume (or any of the exercises in the other volumes), you can repeat each of the exercises again, just as we do in "The *What If?* Writing Group"—which at this writing is well into its fourth year of repetition, with the same students. You'll find that the second, third, and even fourth time around your writing will reach even deeper layers and take you to greater heights. It will be stronger, more compelling and more exciting.

It's a fantastic journey. Plunge into the exercises in **Write It Right: Plot and Dialogue** and experience what it means to really understand the narrative potentials available to you.

The Value of Timed Writing

MOST OF THE EXERCISES in this course are timed. You have a specified amount of time to complete each one, usually 15 or 20 minutes. Thirty at the most. That's it. Period.

Why timed writing? There are two major benefits to timed-limited sessions. As *Natalie Goldman* shows in *Writing Down The Bones*, timed writing exercises force you to keep writing. You have a specific goal and only a short time in which to accomplish it. You have to step out of your way, turn off your inner editor—who is constantly telling you you've used the wrong word, no one will believe that plot, your characters aren't "real" enough, etc.—and simply write. From your heart, from your subconscious instincts, from the place where your stories live. It's authentic writing that's scraped to the bone of emotion. It's compelling and readers will want more.

The second benefit is that you learn to trust yourself and your writing process. When we learn to put our conscious mind on hold and just let the words flow, amazing things happen. Stories emerge that we never knew were there. Connections get made that our conscious minds would never have considered. Best of all, our authentic voice emerges, announcing in clear, ringing tones, "This is who I am as a writer. This is what I need to say." Timed writing exercises will introduce you to yourself.

Timed exercises allow you to step away from your editor self and into your writer self because you don't have time to think. You have to just keep writing, no matter what comes out. It may be hard at first not to go back and correct that word, rethink that action, direct the flow, etc. It takes time to learn to trust your instincts. When you find yourself wanting to go back, don't. *Write* about wanting to go back until you return to the natural flow of the exercise. You can always cut out the extraneous parts later. That's what editing is for.

Timed Writing Format "Rules"

Read the lesson, make sure you understand what to do, then set your timer and write until it dings. Don't stop to think, don't edit as you go, just keep your pen moving or your fingers typing on the keyboard. If you can't think of anything at first, write about not being able to think of anything and just see what happens. Repeat for the next lesson. And the next, and the next...

Also, be aware that my use of the terms "character," "person," "people," "he" and "she" are meant to indicate the protagonists, antagonists and other characters in your stories, whether they be humans, animals or otherworldly creatures. Make whatever adjustments you need to make to each exercise, so that it fits your specific genre and character choice.

Note: An asterisk at the end of an exercise denotes that there is an example of that exercise from my own writing at the end of the section.

Recommended Book List

THESE BOOKS, AMONG OTHERS, have been instrumental in the formation of these lessons. Throughout the course I will reference the pertinent page or pages to read in the appropriate volume. Although you don't need these books to complete these lessons, the information they contain is invaluable. It will add to your knowledge and skills and enhance your learning throughout this series. And they will form a solid foundation for your writer's reference library.

I am listing the copyright year for each volume, so that if you want to read the suggested pages, you will have the correct volume in which to find them. How-to books are often updated with new examples and insights. If you obtain a volume published after the dates listed below, you will still get the same fantastic writing information. But because things will have shifted around in newer editions, you might have trouble finding the proper references for each lesson unless you use a volume with the same publication date as those listed below.

Write Away by Elizabeth George (2004)

What If? Writing Exercise for Writers by Anne Bernays and Pamela Painter (1990)

On Writing by Stephen King (2000)

Characters & Viewpoint by Orson Scott Card (1988)

How to Write a Damn Good Novel by James N. Frey (1987)

The Novel Writer's Toolkit by Bob Mayer (2003)

Finding Your Writer's Voice: A Guide to Creative Fiction by Thaisa Frank and Dorothy Wall (1994)

The 38 Most Common Fiction Writing Mistakes by Jack M. Bickham (1992)

And every writer's library should contain the following reference volumes:

***The biggest dictionary** you can afford (check used bookstores for bargains). There's no substitute for a good, print dictionary

**Roget's Thesaurus*

**Sisson's Synonms* (if you can find it)

**The Elements of Style* (Strunk and White)

**Barron's Essentials of English*

Unit 5: Plot

"Essentially and simply put, plot is what the characters do to deal with the situation they are in. It is a logical sequence of events that grow from an initial incident that alters the status quo of the characters."

~Elizabeth George

PLOT IS PEOPLE IN action. Something happens—the "primary event"—and somebody *must* do something about it. As Elizabeth George puts it, "...plot is what the characters *do* to deal with the situation they are in."

But it can't be just a series of unconnected, random things that the characters do. To be a plot there must be a logical sequence of events based on causality, triggered by the primary event: because that happened, this happens, then this, then this... Because a character did or said something, the status quo changes. The character reacts and things change more. Then the character reacts to those changes. And things continue to change and shift until the situation is resolved.

Therefore, plot is, basically, something that happens to people that **substantially changes their life and/or belief system**, something that cannot be ignored, **and** that has the potential for dire results. Those dire results are called **suspense**, that nail-biting tension that keeps readers wondering if everything really will be okay in the end. Without that essential ingredient, the plot—and the story—will remain flat and uninteresting. Readers will yawn and put the story down.

Without causality, without connection and without tension, the story doesn't have a viable plot.

What gives a story a viable plot? In simplistic terms, it's a through-line or story question, a question that arises at the opening of the story when the primary event occurs, and to which all events and characters are connected until the end, when the question is answered. If your story doesn't have a through-line, it doesn't have a plot. If your story does have a through-line but you don't know what it is, your story is in danger of wandering through a dry, confusing desert hoping to stumble across the plot.

So, what is a through-line? Here are some examples:

Will the boy get the girl? Will the mother save her child's life? Will Mary and Bob stay married? Will Joe get his promotion? Will Audrey defeat the cancer that's invading her body? Will Sherry sleep with Andrew, and if she does, will she end up a pregnant fifteen-year-old? Will Jimmy desert Annie at the altar? Will Herman make it through law school and succeed as a lawyer? Can culinarily-challenged April launch a successful catering business? Will the Orphids invade and destroy the Kendrellan society before Clan Sento fulfills the ancient prophecy?

And from some of my stories: Will Lia remember the truth in time to save her life? (*Tangled Webs*) Will Julie's returning memories spell disaster for her and the man she loves? (*Piece By Piece*) Can the detective figure out where the bodies came from? (*"Hydro-synth"*) Will Marina lose her sanity and freedom because she is too trusting? (*A Matter of Identity*)

Can Mackenzie find the killer and save the young girl's life—and her own? (*Someone Else's Eyes* — in progress) Will Meleia accept or reject her destiny? (*Destany's Daughter*, a YA series in progress)

So, to have a plot, you need characters intimately involved in coping with ever-escalating challenges triggered by a primary event that continues to trigger related events, each more dire than the previous one, until the situation reaches a climax and the problem is resolved.

In a nutshell, **Plot is**:

1. **Characters;**
2. **Primary Event;**
3. **Related Events;**
4. **Suspense;**
5. **Climax;**
6. **Resolution.**

Sounds easy, doesn't it? But, like Point of View (POV), it's easier to understand intellectually than to put into practice. Here in this workbook you will find 8 exercises that will help you assimilate the essentials of plot into your storytelling genes, so that all your stories will pull readers along as they anxiously await the answer to your opening through-line question: Will he…? Will she…? Will they…?

Unit 5, Plot: Contents

Lesson #1: The Rule of Three

THE "RULE OF THREE" is a technique designed to help you find your through-line, the major story question that readers will demand be answered by the last page. It gives you your major plot line onto which all the characters, events and subplots of the story must connect. It's the framework of the story's plot.

The Rule of Three is made up of three elements:

    1. the trigger event,

    2. the basic response of the major character, and

    3. the answer to the story question.

All stories contain this "Rule of Three," no matter whether it's flash fiction or a 1,000 page novel. Without these three elements, all you have is a series of disconnected events and a bunch of characters in search of a plot. Which is a tragedy, both in the writing and in the reading.

The Rule of Three is easy to find in short stories, because there is not much distance between trigger event and resolution. In novels, it becomes harder to see because the straight line from trigger to resolution becomes buried under a large cast of characters and at least one, or perhaps as many as a half-dozen, subplots. The distance between trigger and resolution grows exponentially with every chapter added.

But it is there. And as the writer you have to know what it is and keep it in mind as you write. Even those of us, like me, who write without outlines and only the barest of planning, still need to know the Rule of Three for our books. Otherwise, we can write ourselves into corners that have no relevance to the main story question and find ourselves with no way out. That's a lot of wasted time and effort. Writing's hard enough without wasting any of it.

Look for the Rule of Three in your work, and in every story you read. Learn to recognize it, and you'll soon find it second nature to know the Rule of Three for every story **before** you begin to write it.

READ: *What If?* (Bernays & Painter, 1990) Part IV: Plot, pages 91-92. Then read the Introduction to the first exercise on page 93.

Exercise #1: Three By Three*
(Purpose of Exercise: to learn to craft through-lines)

WRITE DOWN AT LEAST two story ideas. They can be new ones, stories you are thinking of writing, or stories on which you are already working. Now break each story idea into **three, three-word sentences:** beginning, middle and end.

Examples:
Pied Piper: Man lures rats. People won't pay. Man takes children.

Hansel and Gretel: Children get lost. Witch kidnaps children. Children kill witch.

Cinderella: Cinderella can't go. She goes anyway. Cinderella gets Prince.

Someone Else's Eyes: (my in-progress paranormal suspense novel) Woman "sees" killer. Killer kidnaps woman. Woman defeats killer.

The SomeWhen Murder: (my paranormal suspense short story, now being turned into a novella) History captures Skylark. Skylark solves mystery. History releases Skylark.

The key is to hone your three sentences into only **three words each**. This is not as simple as it seems. Choose your words to create the greatest impact. Also, be sure to use **three strong verbs**. Remember, these are the actions that will define the story. Don't get lost in details. The idea here is to find the through-line that will carry the story along regardless of details or characters or subplots.

Set your timer for **10 MINUTES**. If you finish before the timer rings, write out more ideas and the Rule of Three for each of them. Or think of the books you've read recently and write out the Rule of Three for each of them.

Lesson #2: A Variety of Roads to Explore

WE HEAR SO MUCH about plot what it is, what kinds there are, how many different plots exist, etc. It can be overwhelming to try to make sense of what plot is and how to plot, so much so that it often paralyzes writers. They sit at their computers with a blank page on the screen (or with a blank notebook page turned up and pen in hand) with a vague idea in mind, and panic. What do I do now? How do I make this into a tightly-plotted story that an audience will clamor to read?

There is no one right or wrong way to approach plot. If it works for you, it's right. By exploring these various exercises, you can discover what does work best for you: outlining or not outlining, or something in between; working off a vague idea with just a through-line or needing a more organized structure; letting the flow of the story dictate the direction or consciously pushing the direction yourself.

Lesson #2 will help you explore **how to let the story dictate its own direction**. It will help those who start with a great idea and can't figure out where to go from there by giving them a variety of directions from which to choose. It will also help those who tightly outline every movement of a story to loosen up and allow their subconscious room to nudge the events into avenues they might not consciously think of exploring.

Always keep in mind that **the best plots evolve from the story itself**, from the things that happen and the motivations of the characters, whether consciously or subconsciously directed by the writer. Great plots are inextricably tied into what each of the characters wants. They permeate the very atmosphere of the story. Nothing happens that does not grow out of the connection between cause and effect.

This exercise will help you understand that there can be many effects from one particular cause. And that sometimes the first one we choose isn't always the best one for our story's direction.

Exercise #2: Imagining a Variety of Roads to Explore

(Purpose of Exercise: To explore a variety of effects from one cause)

WRITE A SENTENCE OR two that tells how your story begins—the opening action sequence. Don't write the entire scene, just give **a short summary** of what happens in the scene. If you have a story beginning that you don't quite know what to do with, use that story opening for this exercise.

Now write **at least 5 ways** of continuing the story. (If you can think of more, great!) You are not writing the ending of the story. You are simply listing ways you can continue on to the next scene.

Let your imagination run wild. Allow it to go in directions you normally wouldn't go: sci-fi, paranormal, humor, horror, literary, etc. Don't judge the ideas, simply let them flow. The essence of successful brainstorming lies in not rating your ideas as they come, but accepting each one as being as valid as all the rest. Analyzing whether you can use, or are interested in using, them can come later.

Set your timer for **15 MINUTES** and keep listing ideas for your story's next scene until you have at least 5 different ways of continuing the story. If you have time left on the timer when you are done, continue listing more places a new scene could go.

Lesson #3: One Idea, So Much Potential

WHEN WE FIRST GET an idea, our minds start plotting out how the story will unfold: Joe will do this, then Abby will do that, then Jill will go here and Frank will set off for there, until they all meet at the end and everyone lives—changed, yes, and wiser—happily ever after. Or not.

It's exciting. It's invigorating. And it locks us into one version of the story, the very first one our conscious mind devised.

But that might not be the best version of the story. What if Joe did that instead of this? Or Abby went here and Jill did something else? What if Joe weren't even in the story? Or they went their separate ways at the end?

When we rely on our first conscious thoughts, we write good stories. But by getting locked into that first version, we can miss the opportunity to write a really great one. Or the opportunity to take the original seed idea and find out just how many viable, enjoyable stories we could get from it.

The key is the subconscious. Our subconscious minds are always working away behind the scenes, translating everything we see and hear into story fodder. When we allow our subconscious to take over, we can mine those vast silos of ideas and connections to take our stories—and our plots—to the next level.

That's what writers mean when they say, "My characters took over." They didn't lose control of their story. What they did was allow their conscious mind to step aside so their subconscious could spread around some of that creative silage it has been building up for so long.

The subconscious works differently from the conscious mind. The conscious mind deals with outer "reality," with what happens in the here-and-now and how events affect us in our daily lives. But the subconscious has no such constraints. The subconscious removes our personal daily considerations from the equation and lets the story world flow in directions our conscious selves would never consider. It's where science fiction and fantasy come from. It's where ingenious plot twists come from. It's where surprisingly stunning connections happen.

Tapping into the subconscious makes for an amazingly rich story potential that is open to all writers—if they learn how.

READ: *What If?* (Bernays & Painter), Page 106: Introduction, Exercise and Objective

Exercise #3: One Idea, So Much Potential*

(Purpose of Exercise: To explore beyond the first version
of a story idea)

THINK OF A SITUATION, a single event or set of circumstances—such as the one in the reading from Bernays and Painter, a man and woman standing on the sidewalk hailing a cab. Now, write 5 mini-stories (@200 words each) that account for the event or circumstances. Each story should be **different** in plot, characters and theme, even though the situation—hailing a cab—is the same for each one.

You do not have to use hailing a cab for your situation, unless you want to. It is mentioned simply as an example. You can make the situation any one you want it to be, as long as the situation is the same for each of the five mini-stories.

Remember, these are **mini-stories**. Don't get lost in lots of dialogue and detail. The point is to finish each story in the allotted timeframe. For this exercise, it is okay to use narrative to tell the story, as well as shifting emotional omniscience (i.e., moving in and out of the main characters' heads. See *Workbook #2, POV*). The point is to finish each story within the allotted time frame.

Set your timer for **10 MINUTES** and write your first story. When the timer dings, stop, reset it, and start your second story. **Continue in 10 MINUTE SEGMENTS** until you have finished all 5 mini-stories.

Lesson #4: Plot—Let Me Count The Ways

THERE ARE MANY WAYS of working through a plot. The most common, and the one we instinctively gravitate toward, is starting with a given "primary event" and then telling what happens because of it.

But not all plots are created in the same way. Sometimes it can be helpful—and quite creative—to take the end result and write backwards. In other words, **tell how that ending came to be**.

We start by doing the opposite of the "traditional" way of plotting. Instead of asking, "What will the end result be if this happens?" we ask, "What happened to make things the way they are?" It's the way archaeologists figure out what happened in the past. They uncover an ancient city and extrapolate from what they find to discover the way the inhabitants lived, what they believed in, and sometimes even how they died. When we apply this to our stories, we often find some amazing, creative plots evolving without much conscious thought on our part.

The Story Machine, from Perry Glasser, is a heuristic device that juxtaposes two familiar yet unconnected ideas in such a way that they form a new, original idea. It's a great way to learn how to "twist" ideas and plots in fresh ways, because the "twist" has been done for you. All you have to do is figure out how it happened. It's also an invaluable tool for unique, fresh ideas to write about.

It works like this: If you have a list of 5 occupations and a list of 5 actions, you can pair each occupation with each action for a different story (ex: #1 = fashion model, which can be paired with: #1, lets parakeets free, and #2, loosens tennis racket strings, etc., then #2, truck driver, paired with #1, #2, etc.) for a total of 25 ideas to work with. If you have 10 of each, there will be 100 potential stories. 12 of each will yield 144 possible story plots. 20 of each gives you a possibility of 400 story lines! So be sure to add to your listings as new occupations and quirks occur to you. You will never run out of story ideas again.

Exercise #4: Let Me Count The Ways*

(Purpose of Exercise: To work through a plot by knowing the ending beforehand)

Divide your page in half down the middle. On the left side of the page, write **a numbered list** of **at least 10** vocational labels: ex, truck driver, fashion model, doctor, grocery store clerk, etc. Give yourself **5 MINUTES** to do this. Keep listing vocations until the timer dings. You might end up with 10 jobs, or 15 or even 20, depending on how fast you think them up.

On the right side of the dividing line, list **the same number** of mildly strange or unusual behaviors (ex, if you have 10 vocations, you will need 10 behaviors; 15 jobs means 15 unusual actions). Don't be too mundane (ex: washes dishes, brushes the cat) or too melodramatic (strangles lovers, drives flaming truck through prison walls). What you are after is behavior that is a bit off, like loosening tennis racquet strings, or setting parakeets free. Continue until you have the same number of quirky habits as you have vocations, and **make sure to number this list from 1-10** (or however many occupations you listed).

Your page should look like this:

1 Bartender	1 Loosens tennis racquet strings
2 Plumber	2 Sets parakeets free
3 Ballet Dancer	3 Walks backward up driveways

Now, turn your page over. List 1 - 10 (or as many occupations as you have listed on the front) down the left side. To the right of this listing, write down the same numbers in jumbled order, so you have pairs of random numbers. Do not repeat the numbers.

Example: if you have listed 6 vocations and 6 behaviors, you might have a list of pairs like this:

1 - 3
2 - 6
3 - 2
4 - 5
5 - 1
6 - 4

Continue until you have paired all the numbers. Now **circle one pair at random** (ex: 1 - 3), flip the page and look for the first number in the vocation listing (#1 = bartender). Then use the second number of the pair to find the corresponding behavior (#3 = walks backwards up driveways).

Now, write the story of **why this person does this behavior** (ex: Why does the bartender walk backwards up driveways?). Remember, **the behavior is the end of the story**. You task is to add the motivations and actions that culminate with this behavior.

Set your timer for **20 MINUTES** and begin writing your story.

Remember the story potential of this strategy: If you have listed 5 vocations and 5 behaviors, you have a potential of 25 stories. If you have 10 of each, there will be 100 potential stories. 12 of each will yield 144 possible story plots. 20 of each gives you a possibility of 400 story lines. You'll never run out of something to write about with this technique.

Lesson #5: Finding Plots in Your Own Life

OUR OWN LIVES ARE a rich source of plot ideas, a ready source that is often overlooked or ignored. The reason for this is two-fold.

First, most of us think our own lives are dull and boring. (I often say, only half-kidding, that I could make a million bucks by selling my life story as a sleeping pill. And I wouldn't need to write much, because the reader would be sound asleep by about page 2!)

Second, we are afraid of hurting or angering the real people involved in the events that took place. This is a real fear, because friends and family are involved, and some situations can be rather intimate, sensitive or even embarrassing.

But if we can twist the facts out of shape enough, two amazing things happen: the story becomes interesting and fresh, and no one recognizes the original trigger event any more.

The key is in the twist. And the twist comes from asking one simple question, the question that underlies all of fiction: **What if?** (It's such a powerful little question, I chose it for the name of my writing classes: The *What If?* Writing Group.)

Curiosity. It's part of human nature. It's what makes us discontent with what is and makes us wonder about what was or what will be. It's the trigger behind all of society's progress. And it's what spurs all writers on from word to word, paragraph to paragraph, story to story. What if this happened, instead of that? Then what if that happened afterwards? What if he was a she? Sixteen instead of forty-nine? The dog was a cat? The airplane was a train, in the mountains? In Switzerland instead of the American Southwest?

Because the simple question "What if?" triggers both our curiosity and our imagination, our entire life, and the lives of everyone we meet, can become fodder for our stories. We can change out the elements, remove and add players, increase the danger, decrease the familiar and pretty much give what already happened a new lease on life.

Take, for example, my short story titled, "As The Tide Came In." It was triggered by an incident when my adult son was visiting me here in California. We went to Montana de Oro State Park, to Spooner's Cove, to explore the shore of the Pacific Ocean for a while. I had forgotten my sneakers and had on only a pair of flimsy sandals, which made maneuvering over the rocky shore very difficult. So Aaron went off on his own and I ended up standing on the pebbled beach, waiting impatiently while my son had a blast on the rocks at the shoreline.

And I started to wonder, "What If?" What if he wasn't an adult, but a small boy? What if that boy and his mother went to the beach? And what if his mother encouraged this shy little boy to be more adventurous? What if he reluctantly went into a cave near the shoreline? Alone. And what if he didn't come out again?

From twisting something that actually happened completely out of shape, I ended up with a story that won 3rd place in the SLO NightWriters Annual Short Story Contest in 2012.

You will discover from this exercise how easy it is to change and twist events so that the original trigger idea vanishes beneath the fiction you superimpose over it. That allows you to use personal events in a way that is interesting and exciting, and that no one will recognize. You end up with a great story, and peace of mind along with it. The one thing to remember: If other people can still recognize the event that triggered the story, you haven't yet changed it enough.

Once you start working with the events of your life, even the rather ordinary, dull things that happened can become compelling stories with exciting scenes. When you use this exercise, your own life (and the lives of the people you know) can become an almost-unending source of story ideas.

*Exercise #5: Finding Plots In Your Own Life**

(Purpose of Exercise: To use life experiences to trigger plot ideas)

THIS EXERCISE COMES IN four parts. It should take about one hour to complete.

PART A) Think of an episode from your life that resulted in a change of some kind: a change in circumstance, location, relationship, or even your understanding of yourself. Write out what happened in two or three short paragraphs. This is not a story, you don't need dialogue. It's just the basic facts of **what actually happened**.

For example: I was one of the smart nerds in high school and the most popular jock asked me to the prom. I agonized over what to wear, how to act, what to say to him, but on the big day he basically ignored me the entire evening. I was miserable for the entire dance, but didn't have the courage to leave and go home on my own. When he finally dropped me off—without walking me to the door—I decided never to date again. It was 5 years before I accepted another date, preferring to go out in groups only.

Give yourself **10 MINUTES** to complete this step.

PART B) Now ask yourself a series of "What If?" questions concerning this event. You are **not plotting** a story, just exploring the various ways this scenario could be affected by different circumstances.

Using the example in Part A, you might ask:

1. What if the boy stood me up?
2. What if he fawned all over me?
3. What if his friends bet on how long it would be before I kissed him?
4. What if his best friend—who I hated—asked my best friend to the prom, and when we got there the guys switched dates?
5. What if he ridiculed my intellectual abilities?
6. What if he wanted to dance every dance but he was a total spazz? Etc.

You have **15 MINUTES** to complete this portion of the exercise.

PART C) Now pick **one** "What If?" variation and start plotting by asking: What if this happens next? And then this happens? And then this?

For example, from Part B you choose: He's a total spazz and can't dance. You might then ask:

a. What if everyone started mocking both of you because of his dancing?

b. Then what if you could see how bad he feels about being an object of ridicule?

c. Then what if you decide to teach him to dance?

d. Then what if he started to really learn how to dance, and liked it?

e. Then what if you entered both of you in a dance contest? Etc, etc.

Try to come to a climax and an ending to the story. Again, you are not writing a story, just outlining possible scenes/events that could become a story.

Set your timer for **20 MINUTES** and begin writing now.

PART D) Answer the following questions:

1. What are the differences between your fiction story and the real story you started with?

2. What changed and what effect did it have on the original story?

3. How different are the endings?

4. If there are still easily recognizable elements from the real life scenario, how can you twist them even more out of shape?

Give yourself about **10 MINUTES** to analyze the results.

We are often reluctant to use real-life events because we think they are too dull or boring, or we fear hurting or angering the actual people involved in what happened. But you can see from this how easy it is to change and twist events so that the original trigger idea vanishes beneath the fiction you superimpose over it. And that helps you to understand how to use personal events in a way that no one will recognize. You end up with a great story, and peace of mind along with it.

Once you start working with the events of your life, even the rather ordinary, dull things that happened can become compelling stories with exciting scenes. When you use this exercise, your own life (and the lives of the people you know) can become an almost-unending source of story ideas.

Lesson #6: Plots From Odd Situations or Events

MANY STRANGE EVENTS AS well as odd behaviors occur every day in our world. Some things defy explanation—except to a writer with an active imagination. Some are simply things we cannot understand—except for a writer with an active imagination. But all of them offer writers an almost inexhaustible supply of seed ideas from which to concoct plots.

We've all had strange things happen to us, odd coincidences that make us sit up and take notice. How often have you said or thought, "What are the odds of that happening?" when something baffling or amazing happened? It is events like this, as well as even weirder things, that can form the basis of an idea that leads to a marvelous plot.

I remember once, when I was in college, my brother was part of a very successful rowing crew at his high school. They won enough championships to be eligible for the Olympic qualifying trials, which were held in New York City.

My parents and I traveled to New York City that weekend to watch the event (unfortunately, the crew did poorly that day and thus did not qualify for the Olympics). My brother went with his teammates and stayed wherever they were housed, we had no idea where. We stayed in a Manhattan hotel. On Sunday, we debated which church service to attend, then arbitrarily chose the 9:00 am Mass at St. Patrick's Cathedral. This massive structure is football-field huge, with thousands of pews. We walked in, selected a pew and during the service I realized that my brother and some of his crew mates were seated **3 rows directly ahead of us.** What were the odds that we would attend the same service in the same church and sit within 3 rows of each other in that massive building? A very weird coincidence, indeed.

A jaunt onto the internet, or even through local newspapers, will uncover many more strange and intriguing occurrences on which your imagination can chew. Your plots can take you either from the event to a conclusion, or you can work backward using the odd occurrence as the resolution that needs explaining. Either way, you're sure to end up with an intriguing, original plot with which to amaze your readers.

Exercise #6: Plots From Odd Situations or Events

(Purpose of Exercise: To use actual strange events or behaviors to spark plot ideas)

CHOOSE ONE OF THE following odd situations or behaviors and write the story surrounding it. You can work forward from the situation or behavior, or work backward to where it came from. Or any combination of the two. Don't censor your ideas. Just let your mind roam free as you write the "What if?" of your story.

Read the list carefully and choose the one that most appeals to you, or intrigues you most. Then set your timer for **20 MINUTES,** start to write, and see where your subconscious takes your plot. (The following are condensed versions of what appeared in reports on the internet, and the source of each one.)

1. For 3 days in 2009, a total of 28 cattle in the Alps threw themselves off cliffs for no discernible reason, where they plunged hundreds of feet to their deaths. Scientists believe these animals are incapable of committing suicide. (from www.aboutfacts.net)

2. Morning Glory clouds are found all over Australia. They are tubular in shape, hang horizontally and can be up to 600 miles long. Even though scientists have studied them extensively, they have little understanding of how they form or what their purpose is. (from www.aboutfacts.net)

3. In a private home in Belmez, Spain, faces have been appearing for years on the concrete floor of the basement, then vanishing after differing periods of time. The owner's husband tried destroying one face by taking a pickaxe to it and replacing the cement, but then another face appeared in the new cement. (from www.aboutfacts.net)

4. On October 21, 1978, an Australian pilot, flying in clear weather with good visibility, reported a large unidentified aircraft at his altitude. It was illuminated by 4 large landing lights. Air traffic control could see no indication of an aircraft in his vicinity. A few minutes later, the pilot radioed he had engine problems. After brief silence came the last words before pilot and plane vanished without a trace: "It is hovering and it's not an aircraft." (from www.ufo.about.com)

5. The body of an unidentified man was found on a small platform near the top of a 1,000-foot high radio tower. The man wore only a T-shirt and underwear, and there was no sign of violence. No one knows how he got up there or how he died. (from:www.radio.about.com)

6. In Austria in 1885, a cube made of iron, carbon and nickel was found in a coal bed that dates from 12 to 70 million years ago, which puts the origin of the cube in the Tertiary period. The cube appears to have been made by human hands. However, there were no humans on earth during the Tertiary period. (from: www.topsecretwriters.com)

Lesson #7: Plots From Photographs

PHOTOGRAPHS ARE WONDERFUL SOURCES for plot ideas. Some photos tell very clear stories. The tales others tell are more obscure. But when photographs evoke an emotional response, our normal tendency is to make up a story to explain what we see and feel.

Even the most casual snapshot can start our minds spinning. Haven't you ever looked at a picture somewhere and immediately started thinking, "This is what happened," or, "This is what the photo means." The pictures can be of almost anything: people, animals, flowers, forests, mountains, fish, birds, the sea... The list is endless.

The important thing is that the photograph rouses a response in you. It makes you think, makes you want to delve deeper into the images. The picture makes you want to go beyond the images being shown, into a world of your own creation.

That is what imagination means: To **image something into being**, to put down in some form of media (paint, sculpture, music, words, etc.) what you see with your mind's eye. And if your mind's eye can see it, then you can find a through-line with which to craft a plot and then a story.

It all **starts with seeing**. First with your eyes, and then with your mind. Why not let the photographs you take, and those that surround you every day, jump start the process?

Magazines are filled with pictures. Advertising uses photographs. And there are millions of photographic sites online. Check them out. Try Pinterest for one, or Flickr. Scroll through any photographer's website. Or try my website, where a portion of my writing blog is based on photographs: www.SusanTuttleWrites.com/woman of 1000 words.

The perfect "image" is out there, waiting to capture your "imagination" so it can be transformed into an engrossing, enticing story.

Exercise #7: Plots From Photographs*

(Purpose of Exercise: To use photographs to find plots)

TAKE A LOOK AT the following 10 photographs (all used with permission), some of which can be found in color on my website/blog, (www.SusanTuttleWrites.com). In fact, that's how my blog started out: finding characters, settings and story plots in photographs. Check it out and see if any of the pictures inspire you. Just click on the category "Woman of 1,000 Words" and scroll through to see all the photos.

For this exercise, look over the following photographs and choose the one that seems to "talk" to you. Let your imagination supply the colors. Or choose a photo from your own collection, a magazine that's lying around, a catalog you received in the mail, etc. Then write out the story it evokes within you.

Once you select a photo, allow your mind to freewheel as you imagine what the situation could be, what characters might be involved, and how they would react to the changes and challenges presented by the primary event. Don't remain literal: the animals could be humans, or aliens; the setting could be a person or an animal; the humans could be a setting. Let your imagination rule.

When you get an idea, craft a through-line and keep it in mind as you write. Make sure each event grows from the unfolding of the story and keep the tension high as you work toward answering the story question at the climax. Then wrap up all loose ends in the resolution to bring the story to a close.

Give yourself **20 MINUTES** to write this story. Set your timer and begin writing as soon as you choose a picture.

Photo by: Aaron Kondziela

Photo by: James Tuttle

Photo by: Aaron Kondziela

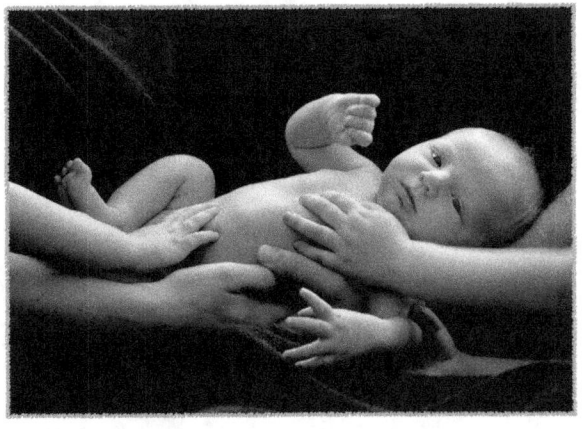

Photo by: Mark Arnold, PhD

Photo by: Susan Tuttle

Photo by: Aaron Kondziela

Photo by: Anna Unkovich

Photo by: Dennis Eamon Young

Photo by: Roland Portillo

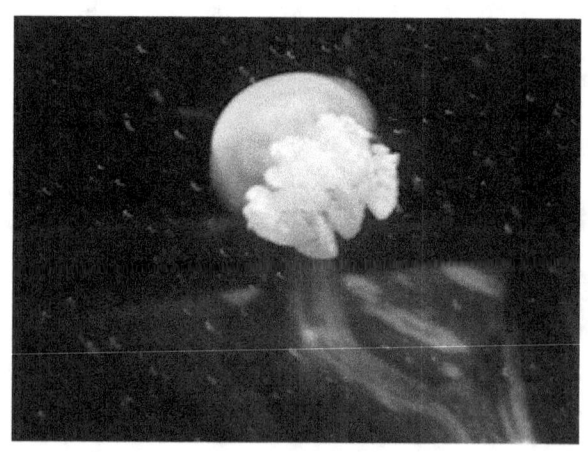

Photo by: Anna Unkovich

Lesson #8: Plots From Overheard Snippets

LISTENING TO THE PEOPLE around you is a great way to mine life for plot ideas. Hearing only snippets of conversations allows your mind to imagine all sorts of ways the few overheard words might fit into a variety of situations. Sometimes they will trigger ideas that work from the phrases forward. Others lend themselves to working backward from the overheard words. Sometimes the words rest in the center of the story. Wherever it ends up, what you overhear can be a gold mine of interesting ideas.

The reason snippets work so well is that you come to them in the middle, or sometimes at the end. You don't know what went before, what the subject matter actually was, what the words really refer to. And you don't know what comes next, what effect these words have on the person listening to the speaker. You have nothing but your imagination to supply those details.

Where do you find these snippets? They're all around you, depending on where you are during the day. Keep your ears open when you walk down a crowded street. As you pass by people who are talking to each other, you can glean a phrase here and there.

People who walk along talking on their cell phones are also great sources, because most of them don't realize they talk loudly enough to be overheard. And since you're walking past them (or they're passing you if you're sitting on a bench), you only get to hear a few words, just enough to spark the imagination.

Another good place to garner odd phrases and words is at meal times. When you are eating by yourself in a restaurant, keep a small notebook and pen on the table so you can write down what you overhear. I usually camouflage this activity with a book. Other diners think I'm reading, but I'm actually eavesdropping, mining for conversational snippets.

And don't forget movies, videos and television. Always keep a notebook and pen handy whenever you watch something. Sometimes a sentence or phrase will pop out at you and set your mind to spinning with "What If?" possibilities. That happened to me when I was watching a rerun of a Buffy the Vampire Slayer episode (yes, I admit it, I'm a Buffy addict!). I don't remember what lead up to it, but what caught my ear was, "...not reenacting scenes from my parents' marriage." I jotted it down, along with the ideas that kept shouting for attention (missed the whole end of that episode), and am now at work on a YA novel titled, "Scenes From My Parents' Marriage," the opening page of which won first place for YA fiction in the Lillian Dean First Page Competition at the Central Coast Writers Conference in 2011.

So keep your ears open for any and all little snippets of conversation you come across each day, and write them down. You never know when one of them will spark just the idea you need to start you writing that award-winning novel or story.

Exercise #8: Plots From Overheard Snippets

(Purpose of Exercise: To use snippets of overheard conversations to generate plot ideas)

BELOW YOU'LL FIND SNIPPETS of conversations I overheard within a two-day period. Read them over and write a story in which one (or more) would appear, either as something one of the characters would say or think, or as part of the narrative. It can be in the beginning, middle or end. Remember that **these words need to arise organically** as part of the plot and action. They can't just be stuck in there because you are supposed to use them.

Read the list, choose a snippet or two, set your timer for **20 MINUTES** and start writing.

Overheard Snippets

...it doesn't work on the subway...
...wish I hadn't told her that...
...he said he'd come by the house at...
...the battle began...
...only if the sun doesn't come out...
...he'll never forgive...

...shouldn't you try harder...
...Jeffrey didn't kill him...
...damn it, it's got to work...
...no one will ever know if...
...she said she'd be here...
...it's going really great on the 16th floor...
...reputations are at stake, you know...
...don't know if I'm coming home...
...she lived on the streets...
...two gentlemen who are...
...whatever and this seat is taken...
...top of my head is going to fall off...
...ten thousand billion billion stars...
...it should arrive by the end...

Examples From My Class Writing

Lesson #1: The Rule of Three

From: ***Stealing Shyon*** (in progress)
Prince kidnaps Queen
Prince usurps kingdom
Queen defeats Prince

From: ***Not Even Death*** (in progress)
Woman seeks closure
Killer covets woman
Woman defeats killer

Lesson #3: One Idea, So Much Potential

Situation: Waiting on a street corner.

Story #1:

Kelly paced back and forth on the sidewalk. Where was Andy? He'd promised to pick them up by 2:30, and now it was quarter to three. If he didn't show up soon, they'd miss the beginning of the movie. And

Selena was crabby enough. Kelly didn't need her throwing a temper tantrum in a crowded theater because she missed the opening scenes of a Disney movie.

Kelly glanced at her watch. Another three minutes gone. She should have known better than to trust her brother. He was so irresponsible. He was always forgetting the things he promised, probably due to the way he drank. She'd caught him more than once with an open beer bottle before nine in the morning. She'd vowed the last time he'd left her stranded at the beach with no way to get home that she'd never trust him again.

But he'd given her those doe eyes of his, that sad puppy-dog look, and begged to be given another chance. Just out of rehab, and making "amends," whatever that meant. Obviously, it didn't mean keeping promises.

It would be better if he wasn't around, if he just went away forever, she thought as a late-model Mercedes pulled to the curb. *It'd be better if he were dead.*

"Kelly. Come on, get in," a deep voice called. "Hurry!"

Uncle Harry? What was Uncle Harry doing here? And why would he care if they were late to a movie? She bundled Selena into the back seat and slammed shut the passenger door.

"Andy's been in an accident, racing to pick you up," Uncle Harry said. "I'll take you to the hospital. It's pretty serious, they're not sure he'll make it. But he begged me to come get you. He didn't want to break his promise. Not when you were the only family member who gave him one last chance."

Pain arrowed through Kelly. She bent her head and prayed, *Please, God, I didn't mean it. Don't let Andy die. Not because of me.*

Story #2:

Jennie stood watching pedestrians hurry to and fro along the hot pavement. Beside her, Billy shuffled his feet and cracked his gum. She put her hand on his arm to still his movement.

"Stop, Billy," she murmured, her voice a mere decibel above the traffic noise. "We don't want to attract any attention."

Billy looked at her, her trusting Downs brother, and grinned. Jennie knew Alex would be angry that she'd brought him today, but their oldest brother, Cliff, had slammed out the door after arguing with his girlfriend on the phone. She couldn't very well leave Billy home alone, could she?

She jingled the car keys in her pocket and glanced again at the storefronts across the street: a small grocer, a bookstore, a shoe repair shop, a small bank branch. Everything looked fine, nothing out of place. She looked at her watch: not long now. They'd better get the car started.

A loud clanging reverberated on the air. The doors of the bank flew open and three men rushed out and raced across the street. Jennie blinked and looked again at her watch. The same time. It had stopped! She looked up just as Alex descended on her.

"Where's the goddamn car, bitch? And what's he doing here?"

Sirens rang in the air, coming closer and closer, as Alex raised his pistol and pointed it at Billy. Jennie stepped in front of her brother.

"No! Alex, please!"

The cops' shouts mingled with the sound of the shot. Fire burst in Jennie's chest. She dropped to the ground. The last thing she saw, as she tried desperately to breathe, was Billy's goofy grin hovering above her.

Story #3:

Cilla reached the corner just as the clock struck midnight. She paused on the walk, then moved back to lean against a concrete column. With her raven hair and black clothing, she knew she blended into the shadows. Unless someone was looking—no, scrutinizing the area—no one would know she was there.

A soft scraping bounced in the air and Cilla tensed, ready to run. Was it Justin? Or Michael? She sidled around to another side of the column, keeping watch on the street, the sidewalk on either side of her, but saw nothing. Then a hand snaked out from behind the column and clamped down on her mouth. A hard arm captured her, pulled her against a hot, sweaty body. A heart tattooed wildly against her back. Cilla's scream jammed in her throat.

"Hush. It's me."

The gentle whisper shivered into her. Relief flooded her and her knees weakened. Only the arms tight around her held her upright.

"Oh, Michael, you scared me!" she whispered back. "I thought it was Justin."

"Does he know?"

"I don't think so. But he suspects something isn't right. He's watched me like a hawk. I almost didn't make it out tonight."

"Then let's go. Now. Tonight. No more chances."

Cilla shook her head. "Not yet. I need more time—"

"We've got enough to fry the bastard," Michael said, cutting off her protest. "You've gone above and beyond already."

Tires screeched as a dark SUV rocketed around the corner at the end of the block. Cilla and Michael looked at each other. Justin! He'd discovered her deception. If he found them there, they'd both die.

Michael took her hand and towed her after him as he raced into a nearby alley, then boosted her over a wrought iron fence. Her pant leg caught on a sharp point and she felt her flesh tear, but she gritted her teeth and ignored the pain as she ran at Michael's side. Her heart swelled with pride. Her first undercover assignment and she'd aced it. One major drug pin going down, a bazillion to go. *Up yours, Dad,* she thought as she labored to draw breath into her tortured lungs and forced her legs to continue running. *This is the right job for me.*

Story #4:

"How much longer?" Dillon asked.

"Shut up!" Jay snarled. He waved his knife in Dillon's face. "You wanna fuck this up, man?"

Dillon shook his head and raised his hands in surrender. Jay was so high, Dillon was amazed he could even see, much less talk or think. No way was he going to get on Jay's bad side, not with the meth coursing in his bloodstream.

They stood in the shadows beneath the awning that arched over the doorway to the video shop. The place had closed hours before. Jay had taken out the nearby street lamps. They'd been here at least two hours already, and still there was no sign of the target. All Dillon wanted to do was go home, forget he knew Jay, forget that Jay owned him.

He kept leaning out from the shadow to scan the street, bouncing on his toes, hands jammed in his pockets, his nerves feeling like fire ants on his skin. Jay yanked him back and slammed him up against the storefront window. The glass rattled. Again, Dillon raised his hands in surrender. Then he stood quietly at Jay's side, waiting.

The shadows at the end of the street moved. Jay tensed. Dillon caught his breath and held it. He could feel his eyes widen as fear coursed through him. His heart thudded as the shadows eddied, bowed, and parted to reveal the slim outline of a woman. Catherine. Walking home from her job at the call center, thinking the street was safe, that her life would continue.

Dillon jammed the side of his hand in his mouth to keep from calling out, warning her. Jay whacked him with the back of his hand.

"Here she comes. Get ready!"

Dillon shoved reluctant fingers in his pocket and pulled out the switchblade. Faint moonlight glimmered on the blade as he pressed the button. He glanced at Jay and they raised their weapons as Catherine stepped closer.

"Cut! Print! That's a wrap," the director yelled. "Steven, you've got Dillon down to a "T." I could read your thoughts in your eyes. That's an Academy Award performance for sure. Good job!"

Story #5:

Deep in Scumville, Condor paused in the shadows that hid the street corner, his gaze scanning the windswept area. Pavement glistened in the aftermath of the nightly rainstorm. Street lamps shed a glowing aura on the wetness, circles of light that merely enhanced the dark that surrounded them. The howl of a scumcat death fight ululated on the air. Nothing moved except ripples in the wetness scraped into motion by the wind. No other sounds rose above its whoosh once the death fight ran its course.

Where was Paygot? Condor had walked past this corner three times already and still the wily caitiff hadn't shown. They were now a half hour past meet-time. Condor would wait no longer. If Paygot wasn't here, that meant the place was no longer safe. Condor believed in the movement, but not as much as he believed in living. Tomorrow had been invented for situations such as this. He'd see Paygot another time.

He turned to leave then caught movement at the corner of his eye. He faded into the deepest shadows and watched through half-lowered lids as an unmarked aircart glided to a stop a few feet away. Condor held his breath. He knew that if he didn't move a hair, they'd never see him. He slowly parted his lips to draw silent shallow unnoticeable breaths.

A man descended from the driving area of the aircart, and sauntered down the street to Condor's left. An Enforcer, or a Mind Molder, Condor knew. No one else was heavily armed enough to saunter in Scumville. The man reached the corner and turned, ambling back the way he'd come. A slight lift of his chin made Condor slowly swivel his eyes to the right. A second man marched along toward the first, leading a young woman. Sixteen? Seventeen? No more than that. Condor almost gasped as he recognized her face when she passed beneath a street light.

The two men passed, then the first turned and grabbed the girl, muffling her scream with his hand. The first man folded to the ground. Condor heard the sharp ring of ankle shackles ratcheting shut. The two men carried the struggling girl to the aircart. The rear doors opened and they tossed her to waiting hands. One short scream split the night, cut off by the sound of a hand hitting flesh. Then the doors closed, the first man regained the driving compartment and the second marched on and vanished into the night.

Condor stood still for a few more minutes until the aircart vanished. He needed to leave the city. Now, without delay. Things were about to get mega-dangerous, very fast. If he was not mistaken, the Governor's only daughter had just been kidnapped.

Lesson #4: Let Me Count The Ways

My Occupations:

1. Cupcake baker
2. Priest
3. Talk show host
4. Housewife
5. Banker
6. Contractor
7. Painter
8. Pet store owner
9. Gardener
10. Jewelry Maker
11. Bus driver
12. Police officer
13. Detective
14. Attorney
15. Writer
16. Teacher
17. Professor
18. Editor
19. Agent
20. Publisher

My Behaviors:

1. Eats sausage every Thursday
2. Collects angels with broken wings

3. Wears a ring on each finger

4. Gardens in high heels

5. Drinks wine with chocolate

6. Reads only used paperbacks

7. Collects candy bar wrappers

8. Eats peanuts outside only

9. Won't step on sidewalk cracks

10. Collects yarn he/she never uses

11. Wears two watches

12. Reads only comic books

13. Writes with a fountain pen only

14. Brushes his/her hair 1,000 strokes a day

15. Hangs paintings upside down

16. Collects cuckoo clocks that keep the wrong time

17. Puts lunch money in the alms box

18. Burns only black candles

19. Cooks on a wood stove

20. Wears cat-shaped glasses with rhinestones

My random pairing of numbers:

1.	11
2.	3
3.	7
4.	14
5	10
6	2
7	17
8	**1 = choice for story**

9	5
10	19
11	20
12	9
13	16
14	4
15	18
16	8
17	6
18	15
19	12
20	13

8 = Pet store owner

1 = Eats sausage every Thursday

Pet Emporium Story:

Oscar Hamlin bustled around his store with his usual bounce-footed gait, straightening a shelf here, wiping away dust there. He paused at each cage to coo at the inhabitants: gerbils and mice; dogs and cats; tropical fish, birds and lizards. Most of these creatures had been in residence for long years. Oscar's Pet Emporium, tucked into a little-traveled part of town, was seldom visited by the outside world.

The animals reacted to his voice, his bubbly presence, with responses that would have amazed onlookers, had there been any. Mice and gerbils chittered at him. Lizards remained motionless as he stoked their leathery backs, the Gila turning its head to touch the back of Oscar's hand. Puppies and kittens climbed over each other in their eagerness to receive his caresses. Even the fish followed his finger along the glass of their tanks, their mouths moving in aquatic kisses against the hard surface.

"Oh, my lovelies," Oscar crooned as he bounded over to turn the sign to 'closed,' "another week has passed. And all my favorites still here. Haven't we had fun?"

He turned around and spread his arms, encompassing the whole interior of the crowded room.

"It's Thursday," he said. "Whose turn is it this week?"

The kittens mewed as though they understood his words. Puppies whined their response. Rodent wheels spun and bird chirps echoed in the huge space. In the 50-gallon tank in the corner, a triangular head raised above the dun rocks and swayed. Oscar nodded.

"Luther. Yes, I do believe you're right. It's your turn today."

Oscar walked over to the tank and lifted out the twelve-foot snake. He stood holding it, nose to nose, as Luther's tongue flickered, tasting Oscar's scent. Then it moved, slithered around Oscar's neck and settled in for the journey into the back room.

They ducked through a beaded curtain and entered a world draped with middle eastern tapestries, dimly lit with colorful hanging lanterns and furnished with floor pillows. Oscar hummed an Indian-flavored tune as he moved to the small kitchenette in the far corner. There he pulled out a mixing bowl, a frying pan, a large carving knife. From the refrigerator he chose a juicy garlic head, then took down an assortment of spices from an overhead cupboard.

"It's important, Luther, to make sure everything is balanced just so. You're giving me such a precious gift. I must make sure that I honor you fully."

He glanced at his image in the small mirror that hung beside the work space. His tiny eyes sparkled with kittenish playfulness. His ginger hair resembled gerbil fur more than human hair. His head moved with the abrupt suddenness of an alert squirrel, and his eye caught the profile of his bird-beak nose.

He gestured to Luther. The snake slid from his shoulders onto the work space. Oscar stroked its head; Luther's tongue stroked the back of Oscar's hand. Then Oscar picked up the cleaver and gutted the snake. He diced the meat, mixed it with the spices and garlic, then stuffed the sausage mixture in the casings. He fried the sausage, his mouth watering from the delicious aroma, then plated his dinner and carried it to the table.

"Thank you, Luther, for joining with me in essence and life," Oscar intoned as he carefully cut into the sausage. His eyes closed in bliss at the first taste. As he continued to eat, Oscar's skin took on the sheen of dry leathery scales and he knew he'd survive for one more week.

Lesson #5: Plots from Life Experiences

Situation: When I was in college I studied Theater. I majored in acting and directing. My best friend was a girl named Lizbeth. My boyfriend's name was Tony. Tony was a musician, and since I also am a singer, we spent a lot of time together with music. He used to play songs to me over the phone to tell he how he felt about me. Sometimes he never said a word, just played music whose lyrics supplied the emotion. It was romantic beyond my wildest dreams.

He would pick me up from rehearsals late at night, when the buses stopped running, and take me home. One night he offered to take Liz home, too, since her car had broken down and she had no way to get home. It became a ritual: He'd pick us both up, drop Liz off, then take me home. We'd kiss and talk for about an hour before I'd go in the house. I was having problems with my parents at the time and he was very supportive and loving. It wasn't until about 6 months later that I discovered that after he left me, he'd go back to Liz and spend the night with her. She had never said a word to me, just acted as though everything was the same as always, and the whole time she was sleeping with Tony. I was devastated by this betrayal and it took me years before I trusted another woman—or a man—with any deep part of myself.

What If Listing:

Liz came and confessed that Tony had hit on her?

What if she told another friend who then told me?

What if Tony said Liz had hit on him and he'd turned her down?

What if Tony was going to Liz's house because he liked her brother?

What if Tony's best friend called to tell me?

What if Tony's best friend met me to tell me and he fell in love with me?

What if I let Liz have Tony and I went after another friend's boyfriend?

What if Liz confessed to me, we worked it out and decided we loved each other?

What if I got my brother and his friends to beat up Tony and Liz?

What if I sabotaged Tony's car and they were in an accident?

What if Tony and/or Liz died in the accident?

What if, in playing around with paranormal spirit circles, a "spirit" told me about Liz and Tony?

What if I learned about Liz and Tony in a seance and then became a famous medium, specializing in wrecking relationships?

What if I poured all my hurt into my next role and a scout saw the performance and I got a Broadway/Hollywood contract?

What if I posted Tony's picture on the internet with a description of what he'd done?

What if I posted Liz's picture with a description of what she'd done?

What if I started a campaign of poison-pen letters to drive Liz crazy?

What if I left school and entered a convent?

Plot Building: What Iffing the What Ifs...

I chose: What if I sabotaged Tony's car and they were in an accident and Tony was hurt, Liz killed?

What ifs:

What if my other friends suspected I had something to do with the accident?

What if the police also believed it, but had no evidence?

What if my mother forced me to go to Liz's funeral and I started to really feel the guilt?

What if Tony was handicapped because of the accident?

What if guilt forced me to drop out of school?

What if I got a job as a counselor at a crisis hotline, trying to help others who had been hurt like I was?

What if Tony turned to me in his sorrow?

What if Tony fell back in love with me and asked me to marry him?

What if I went along with this to make up to him for what I did?

What if we got married and had kids?

What if Tony wanted to name our first girl after Liz?

What if I couldn't love the child because of her name?

What if I started drinking to drown the increasing guilt I felt?

What if I started resenting Tony for reminding me of what I'd done every time I looked at him?

What if I neglected the kids because of the drinking?

What if Social Services was called in?

What if I lost the kids because I was out of control?

What if Tony and I got divorced and I lost visitation rights?

What if I kidnapped the kids and then got into an accident and Lizzie was hurt?

What if I then realized I had to take responsibility and turned myself in to the cops?

Lesson #7: Plots from Photographs

I found a wonderful photo of muddy boots on a hiking gear website that sparked my imagination. All you can see in the picture is the bottom of mud-spattered trousers and the mud-caked boots, standing on rough grass and weeds. Here are the two plots I devised from this photo:

Story #1:

Place: a small village surrounded by rainforest deep in the Brazilian jungle.

Main Character: A man, the leader of the village, whose only son, age 4, was kidnapped from his bed at night. He suspects it was a rival leader from a nearby village who has coveted the wealth his village enjoys from a secret source of gold and gemstones hidden deep in the jungle. The man had been out searching in the surrounding forest for clues, which is why his pant legs and boots are covered with mud. All he found was a large coin, not one familiar to him or the area where the story takes place.

While he was searching he received a message, purportedly from the kidnappers, via a young autistic boy who cannot be questioned, that he is to meet someone at the fountain and give that person the coin. He will then be told what he needs to do to bring his son home. Any attempt to interfere with the kidnappers will result in the boy's death. The man is sure that whoever took his son did so to force him to reveal the location of the secret cavern where the gold and gems are found. Can he recover his son successfully without revealing the source of his village's prosperity?

Story #2:

Place: a planet far from Earth

Main Character: a woman, heir to the throne of Meroc, was abducted and left to fend from herself on a distant planet, so the pretender could ascend the throne and rule in her place. She was forced to don men's clothing, which is forbidden for women to wear on her planet, and was left, unconscious and without shoes, in the middle of a desert. When she woke she stumbled through burning sands, eventually coming across a dead body, whose boots she took after wrapping her injured feet in shreds of his clothes.

She eventually found an oasis that was half swamp and waded through it to reach a hamlet in the center of the oasis, which is deserted. No sign of habitation anywhere, as though all inhabitants had vanished in the night. In the center of the oasis is a fountain, and in the fountain she discovered a large silver disc with strange runic symbols carved into it.

It is the only clue she has to where she is, or who the people once were. In the wind she can hear echoes of voices, and the thunder of laser blasts coming closer and louder. Something ominous is drawing nearer and nearer. Can she survive what is coming her way, survive the encounter, and find her way through the desert and back to her own planet in time to save her people from the usurper?

Unit 6: Dialogue

"(While) realistic dialogue is one of the most powerful tools at a writer's disposal, nothing pulls the reader out of a story faster than bad dialogue."

~Ginny Wiehardt

DIALOGUE. WHAT IS IT?

Easy. Dialogue is two or more characters talking to one another.

Like I said, easy, because we all talk to each other, every day. Some of us talk more than others. So, how hard can it be to put down on (real or virtual) paper the words that come out of our characters' mouths? Gotta be second nature, right?

Wrong.

Dialogue is not simply two or more characters talking to each other. If it were, we'd bore our readers—and ourselves—practically to death. Imagine what would happen if we took dialogue straight from "real" life:

Joe is getting ready to pick up his daughter when he gets a call. He answers the phone on the third ring.

"Hello?"

"Hi. Is Joe there?"

"Yes, this is Joe speaking."

"Hi, Joe, this is Mandy."

"Oh, Mandy. I didn't recognize your voice. Um, how are you?"

"I'm fine. And you?"

"Great, great. How's your dad? I heard he's been sick."

"Yes, he was, you know, but now he's better. It's been a tough winter."

"I know what you mean. We've all been passing the flu back and forth around here ourselves. I'm glad the weather is starting to warm up."

"Yeah, I know what you mean."

"Um, you know, it's been a long time since we've seen each other. We should have lunch or something. You know, sometime soon."

"I'd really like that. And, um, you should bring Martha with you. She must be almost all grown up by now."

"Thanks for thinking of her. It's been hard since her mom died. And now that she's a teenager, it's even harder. She could use, um, another woman to talk to, you know?"

"Funny to think of her as a woman. But you're right, it would be good for her. I can't wait to see her again."

"How about Saturday the 12th? We could meet at Denny's for lunch. Um, ah, bring Bill, too, if he wants to come."

"Bill and I, um, we broke up, you know? About six months ago."

"Gosh, I'm sorry to hear that. I liked the guy, thought he was good for you, you know. Uh, what happened?"

"I don't want to talk about it."

"I hear you. What a bummer for you. Hey, great to talk to you, Mandy, but I've got to go. Uh, gotta pick Martha up from, you know, gymnastics."

"Okay, I'll see you at Denny's on Saturday. Um, around one?"

"Sounds perfect. See you then."

"Oh, wait, before we hang up. Ah, here's why I called...."

And by then, if they haven't put the book down (and we haven't lulled ourselves to sleep and never finished writing the phone call, much less the book) our readers' eyes are crossed. Their minds are numb. They want to strangle both Joe and Mandy. And we're just getting to why she called, which is the whole point of the conversation!

Ever notice how, even though the dialogue sounds perfectly natural, in movies and on television characters rarely say more than one "hello" when answering the phone—if they say hello at all—don't exchange inane pleasantries and never say good-bye? They get right to the point and then hang up. No asking about the kids, Jack's promotion, Annie's new carpeting. They say what needs to be said to further the story, then end the conversation. The same happens when they talk in person. Nothing extraneous, not like in real life.

If you doubt that dialogue in real life is fairly dull, boring and inane a lot of the time, (secretly) tape record a conversation with one of your friends or acquaintances (or between two of your friends) and play it back for yourself. You'll be amazed at how many incomplete sentences, digressions, "ums," "you knows" and other such expressions you will hear. And at how long it takes to get to the point, how often you interrupt each other with unconnected thoughts. We all do it. It's subconscious; we don't realize it or even hear it at the time.

But we can't do that with dialogue in our stories. It has to **sound** like natural speech but it **can't be** natural speech. Or we'll turn off our readers.

So, once again, what is dialogue?

Dialogue is two or more people speaking to each other in a way that approximates normal speech. It sounds like the way people talk, but it isn't. It doesn't ramble. It doesn't include inconsequentialities. Or non-sequiturs. Or information that isn't germane to the story.

Always keep the following in mind when working with dialogue: Everything the characters say must pertain to the story in some way. **All dialogue must**:

1. **Impart information,**
2. **Reveal character,**
3. **Illustrate the nature of a relationship**
4. **Advance the plot,**
5. **Increase tension/suspense, and/or**
6. **Control pacing.**

And it must **sound normal and natural** while doing all the above.

The 8 exercises that follow will help you understand how dialogue operates in literature. As you work through them you will hone your skills so that your dialogue floats naturally from the mouths of your characters while doing its main job with aplomb: Advancing the story.

Unit 6, Dialogue: Contents

Lesson #1: Avoid Talking Heads

HAVE YOU HEARD THE term "Talking Heads"? It's often used to refer to newscasters who sit behind a bland backdrop and read their bits of news items into the camera lens with fairly blank looks on their faces. There is no setting, no action, no other characters to take attention from what they say, not even any hand gestures, just a torrent of words streaming from their mouths.

It's hard at times to concentrate on what they say, difficult not to let your mind wander when all there is, is words. And it's usually a relief when the program cuts in with an action shot of the latest fire, office dedication ceremony or traffic jam. There's finally something to look at that makes what the newscasters say seem real, connected and of more import.

Talking Heads also occur in books and stories when the author forgets to anchor the conversation in the world that surrounds the characters. Just like in real life, things don't stop when two people start talking. The environment doesn't disappear. The car they are riding in continues down the street, and if one is driving he or she continues to turn the wheel and work the pedals. If dinner is cooking, there will be stirring to do, a table to set, an oven to check. Speakers shrug, scratch their cheek, play with their hair or other objects, look away and/or down, pace the room, etc. **Life continues while characters talk.**

Think of what happens on stage during a play, or on screen during a movie or TV program. The actors don't just talk on a blank stage or screen, without facial expressions and body movements. They are engaged in some kind of action which is set in a particular environment. All the elements of the scene work together to impart knowledge to the viewer. Nothing is extraneous, just stuck in there for 'color.' Even screen- and stage plays note on their pages the other necessary elements of the scene besides the conversation.

When we put a conversation on paper, we won't have those visual clues unless we put them in along with the words the characters speak. Without a thorough grounding in the setting, readers can forget where the characters are and lose track of the story line. If readers can't visualize the setting and the action, they lose interest and have trouble concentrating on the words being spoken. And that leads to putting down the story, unfinished. Not something any writer wants to happen.

How do you avoid Talking Heads? By inserting such things as dialogue tags, action bits, internal dialogue and setting.

1. **Dialogue tags** are simply 'said.' "Joe said" or "Mandy said." It attributes dialogue. In other words, it tells readers who is speaking the words.

2. **Action bits** are just what it says, a bit of action committed by the speaker that lets the reader know who is speaking. Action bits ground the reader in the scene and can also be used to show character or give clues to future events.

3. **Internal thoughts** are the silent musings of the POV character which, while showing readers who is speaking, also shows them character and motivation.

4. **Setting** is the place where the conversation is taking place, which grounds readers in the reality of the story and reinforces the impact of the information being imparted.

The key to avoiding Talking Heads, then, is to continue to show the action, the motivation and the setting **while the characters are speaking**. Where they are talking is important. What they are doing while the conversation unrolls is important. What the POV character is thinking can be equally vital. It all works together to give readers a complete, compelling picture that pulls them along until the story ends.

Exercise #1: Avoiding Talking Heads*

(Purpose of Exercise: To ground dialogue within a scene)

THIS EXERCISE CONSISTS OF three parts. It should take you from about 45 minutes to an hour to complete.

Part A: Create a scene between two characters, one of whom wants something: information, to borrow something, to dissuade the other person, to convince the other person, whatever. This is not an all-out argument, just dialogue between two people who know each other fairly well.

Make the issue something personal to them (ex., one wants to have a baby, the other doesn't; landlord and tenant can't agree on lease terms; they've decided to shoplift and one is getting cold feet.) Do not use any tags or bits, not even he said/she said. No indication of tone of voice, no action, no setting. Just dialogue, like in a play.

These two should be Talking Heads only, just like the example in the Introduction (page 55-56). No tags, bits, internal thoughts or setting. Dialogue only.

Give yourself **20 MINUTES** to write this scene, starting now.

Part B: Re-write the same scene using dialogue tags, bits, internal thoughts (of the POV character) and scene settings. Have at least one character involved in some kind of activity that may or may not be related to what they are talking about: cooking dinner; repairing something; cleaning something; playing solitaire; doing exercises; painting or drawing or other hobby; gardening; giving someone a haircut, etc. Use that activity to help readers stay attuned to who is saying what.

For example, take a part of the scene used in the Introduction (of course, a real scene would start with why Mandy called and go from there). Here is what it might look like with tags, action bits and setting included:

"I'd really like that," Mandy said.

Her voice sounded a bit distant, not as warm and vibrant as he remembered. Joe could hear a clicking noise in the background, like a pencil bouncing on a desktop. Mandy always did that when she got nervous. He wondered what was going on in that lovely head of hers.

"And," Mandy's voice speeded up, as though she was trying to convince herself and not just him, "you should bring Martha with you. She must be almost all grown up by now."

"Thanks for thinking of her." Joe looked at the picture of his 'two girls' on the wall, the one taken just before the accident that snatched Jane from them. After all these years, it still hurt to look at Jane's picture. "It's been hard on Martha since her mom died. And now that she's a teenager, it's even harder. She could use another woman to talk to, you know?"

He blinked tears from his eyes as Mandy's voice echoed on through the receiver, still rapid and a bit brittle.

"It's strange to think of her as a woman, I keep picturing her as a little girl. But you're right, it would be good for her to have a woman to talk to. I can't wait to see her again."

Should I get together with her? Joe wondered. Am I ready for more than friendship, if that should happen? He stretched the phone cord across the room and checked the calendar that clung to the refrigerator, smiling at all the notations in Martha's curlicue writing: band practice on Monday, gymnastics today, dinner with Nana on Wednesday, movie with Carley on Friday. The only notation for him was a parent-teacher conference at the end of the month. A pang of loneliness shot through him. Maybe getting together wouldn't hurt. Much.

"How about Saturday the 12th?" he asked, his trembling fingers picking up the pen that dangled from a string beside the calendar. "We could meet at Denny's for lunch."

There. A nice, neutral place and his daughter for a buffer. He could survive that. Right?

Don't just stick tags, action bits, internal thoughts and setting references in willy-nilly. Analyze your original dialogue as you write. Ask yourself: Does it all still fit into a scene that has action and setting included? If not, what should be left out and why? Does any of it need to change? If so, why? For what purpose?

Set your timer for **20 MINUTES** and begin writing.

Part C: Now ask yourself, which was easier for you to write: dialogue only (Talking Heads), or a full scene with tags, bits, internal thoughts and setting? Write out why one was easier than the other for you. Which gives a fuller picture of what is happening? Which do you think is more compelling for the reader, and why? Give yourself **5 MINUTES** to answer these questions.

Though it's more work, the full scene should be easier to write because character can be revealed through tags, bits, action and internal thoughts as well as dialogue. The entire scene is not carried only by what the characters say, but also by how they react to what is being said and how they use the environment to enhance or deny what is being said. And that certainly gives the writer more to work with in crafting a full, realistic conversation. If you found straight dialogue easier to write, you may be a budding playwright!

Lesson #2: It Ain't What You Say, It's How You Say It

ONE OF THE KEYS to effective dialogue is making each character's speech unique and distinct. That means knowing each character's background and place of origin. It's knowing that New Englanders say 'pahk the cah' for 'park the car' and Southerners say 'y'all' for a plural 'you.' (But not for the singular form.) It's knowing that in different parts of the country people call the same thing by a different name. For example, a Chef Salad in most parts of the U.S. is called a Julienne Salad in Western New York, while a Western N.Y. Chef Salad is merely a small Dinner Salad elsewhere in the country.

Part of the distinctness of speech is the **way** we talk. Certain areas and cultures have specific speech fragments that are unique to their origins. Sometimes it comes from English being a second language in which the parts of sentences are arranged differently from the way they are in the person's native language.

My pastor at church is from Mexico, and his English often puts the object before the verb, especially when asking a question, they way it would be structured in Spanish. Thus, he would say, "What he is doing?" instead of "What is he doing?" Definitely a unique, distinct speech pattern all his own.

Think of the way people from other countries speak English. The differences are more than just the accent. They are also the way the words are put together, or sometimes the way words are left out. English liberally uses 'the,' 'a' and 'an,' though many other languages do not, which lends a distinctly recognizable pattern to the way the foreign language is translated into English words.

Pronunciation also affects the uniqueness of a person's speech. I have a writer friend who we always tease because he still retains what we call his "Brooklyn-ese." He can't say 'un.' He pronounces it 'on.' So instead of saying, 'She was unsteady on her feet," he says, "She was onsteady on her feet." His way of speaking marks him as a native of Brooklyn, New York.

But using too much fancy spelling to denote odd pronunciations can lead to confusion for both the writer struggling with consistent phonetic spelling and the reader who is trying to interpret what the oddly spelled words mean. The easiest way to let readers know who your characters are and what type of environment they are from is to use **speech fragments**.

Speech fragments give a unique flavor to a character's speech and hint at background and/or place of origin. They convey a sense of accent (without resorting to phonetic spelling) or national, regional, class, race and/or cultural differences. Widely familiar foreign words (in *italics*, always) or names can help establish character distinctions, also.

Consider these speech fragments from famous published works:

"My mamma dead. She die screaming and cussing." ~Alice Walker, *The Color Purple*

" 'I won't keep you,' I says. 'You must get a job for yourself.' But sure, it's worse whenever he gets a job; he drinks it all." ~James Joyce, "Ivy Day in the Committee Room"

"*Muy buenos*," I said. "Is there an Englishwoman here? I would like to see this English lady.'
"*Muy buenos*. Yes, there is a female English." ~Ernest Hemingway, *The Sun Also Rises*

All in all, Harry Laines' wedding was one of the worst events in my experience, tragic in society. ~Nancy Lemann, *Lives of the Saints*

"...the working mens one Sunday afternoon taking they only time off. They laying around drinking some moonshine, smoking the hemp, having a cock fight." ~Peter Leach, "The Convict's Tale"

You can see that the way the words are put together allows the reader to "hear" the accent, the background, the educational level, even the country of origin of the characters. All without creative spelling or an inordinate number of dropped letters. Readers will intuitively understand, after reading, "My mamma dead," that the 'g' on screaming and cussing is not articulated. And the rhythm of the words in the Joyce quote clearly denotes an Irish brogue.

Creating speech fragments for your characters is the easiest, most sure way to show their distinctive traits and backgrounds. And your readers will thank you for not confusing them with impossible-to-read spellings or a plethora of apostrophes denoting dropped letters.

*Exercise #2: It Ain't What You Say, It's How You Say It**

(Purpose of Exercise: To reveal uniqueness of speech)

WRITE AT LEAST FIVE speech fragments of your own. Keep in mind that the objective in writing speech fragments is three-fold:

1. To reveal character
2. To convince the reader by making the dialogue sound credible
3. To add variety

You can write these fragments for characters in stories you are working on, or for characters you make up for this exercise. Write one speech fragment per character and make each as distinct as you can.

Give yourself **12 MINUTES** for this exercise. If you get to number 5 before the timer runs out, continue writing more speech fragments until it dings.

Differences in speech aren't just realistic. They are interesting and provocative and they can give vitality to your story. Remember: Speech without flavor is like food without savor.

Lesson #3: Writing For Your Audience

AS WRITERS, WE WANT the widest audience we can attract. But because of the dual nature of the major root words in English, the words we choose can affect who will read and enjoy our writing. And it will affect the words our characters use when they talk, depending on their upbringing and educational background.

English takes its roots from many languages, but the two most common are Anglo Saxon and French/Latin. These were the two major languages spoken by the common people and the aristocracy in old England. Most words that have other root origins have been added to basic English over the years.

Anglo Saxon was the language of the common people. Its words are earthy, simple and direct. It is the language of an illiterate people, those who worked hard for a living and rarely mastered the art of reading or writing.

French and Latin were the languages spoken by the aristocracy, the highly educated idle class, who passed the time not working but engaging in philosophical and theological discussions. They were both considered elevated languages spoken by those of influence and education.

As modern English evolved, it took its roots from both of these classes, the educated and the uneducated. That is what gives our language such richness, and such a wealth of options for written expression. But not understanding the proper words to choose can lead to a rough feel to our narrative, leaving the reader with the impression something is not quite right, a lingering sense of vague confusion. And in the mouths of our characters, the wrong root words can destroy—or the right ones enhance—their carefully crafted backgrounds.

For a wide audience, writers need to blend both the Anglo Saxon and French/Latin root words carefully so that they maintain a smooth flow. For a more educated audience, the French/Latin roots should dominate. And for an audience not as versed in higher education, use mostly Anglo Saxon root words.

The same holds true for our characters. A highly educated professor at an Ivy League college would tend to speak in elevated French/Latin terms. Someone who quit school in ninth grade would probably veer almost exclusively to the Anglo Saxon version of the words. A self-taught character might be able to blend the terms smoothly with only occasional lapses, while someone simply pretending to be more educated might choose all the wrong French/Latin root words at the wrong time, and end up sounding even more ignorant and stilted. That could either enhance or destroy the credibility of the character depending on how you have crafted him/her.

*Exercise #3: Writing For Your Audience**

(Purpose of Exercise: To explore the differences in English root words)

THIS IS A TWO-PART exercise. It should take you around a half hour to complete.

Part I: Randomly choose at least **15 word pairs** from the listing below. Then write a few short paragraphs, using as many of the circled Anglo-Saxon (AS) words as you can. What you write can be an introduction to a story, a scene from a story, an opinion piece, etc. Doesn't matter, as long as you incorporate the chosen Anglo/Saxon words into the narrative. Be sure to underline the given words as you use them, so you can recognize them easily for Part II.

Give yourself **15 MINUTES** to write this short piece, using as many of the Anglo-Saxon words you circled as you can, preferably all of them.

Part II: When the timer dings, stop, reset your timer and rewrite the piece, using the French/Latin words in place of the Anglo-Saxon words. You may need to do a bit of re-writing to make the French/Latin words work smoothly into the piece. A more educated vocabulary often requires a more sophisticated sentence structure. Give yourself **10 MINUTES** to do this.

Read the two pieces once you have finished them. You'll find the difference these root words can make in the feel of a piece quite interesting. And you'll have a better understanding of which words to choose for your characters when they open their mouths and speak. (A good dictionary is a tremendous help in choosing the right words. Always purchase the largest one you can afford, and use it often.)

(Key):

AS = Anglo-Saxon	**FL** = French/Latin
AS = Woman	FL = Female
AS = Happiness	FL = Felicity
AS = Hut	FL = Cottage
AS = Bill	FL = Beak
AS = Friendship	FL = Amity
AS = Dress	FL = Clothe
AS = Help	FL = Aid
As = Folk	FL = People
AS = Hearty	FL = Cordial
AS = Holy	FL = Saint
AS = Deep	FL = Profound
AS = Lonely	FL = solitary
AS = Love	FL = Charity
AS = Begin	FL = Commence
AS = Hide	FL = Conceal
As = Feed	FL = Nourish
AS = Inner/Outer	FL = Interior Exterior
AS = Leave	FL = Abandon
AS = Die	FL = Perish
AS = Mouth	FL = Oral
AS = Nose	FL = Nasal

AS = Eye

AS = House

AS = Book

AS = Moon

AS = Sun

AS = Watery

AS = Town

As = Kingly

AS = Youthful

AS = Wretched

AS = Same

AS = Share

AS = Manly

AS = Tale

AS = Cold

AS = Heavenly

AS = Darling

AS = Half

AS = Look for

AS = Put out

AS = Hinder

AS = Sleeplessness

AS = Give/Hand

AS = Freedom

AS = Come near

AS = Up

AS = Murder/Killing

As = Weighty

FL = Ocular

FL = Domicile

FL = Literary

FL = Luna

FL = Solar

FL = Aquatic

FL = Urban

FL = Regal

FL = Juvenile

FL = Miserable

FL = Identical

FL = Portion

FL = Virile

FL = Story

FL = Frigid

FL = Celestial

FL = Favorite

FL = Semi

FL = Search

FL = Extinguish

FL = Prevent

FL = Insomnia

FL = Present/ Deliver

FL = Liberty

FL = Approach

FL = Ascend

FL = Homicide

FL = Ponderous

Lesson #4: Idioms Make It Real

IDIOMS ARE A GREAT way to add a distinctive flair to your characters' speech.

Idiom comes from the Latin word *idioma*, meaning "special property," by way of the Greek *idios*, meaning "one's own." It denotes an expression that is not literal, but rather figurative. In other words, the meaning of the word or phrase is dependent on a common understanding rather than taken from the words themselves.

Here are a few of today's commonly used idioms, to give you a fuller idea of what an idiom is:

Pull one's leg
Take to the cleaners
Drop a line
Keep an eye out
Keep one's head above water
Break a leg
See a man about a dog
Kick the bucket
Cut from the same cloth

Feather-brained
Sick as a dog
Down in the dumps
Piece of cake
Raining cats and dogs

As you can see, the understood meaning of an idiom is completely different from what the words actually say. When you tell someone to "break a leg," you mean *good luck, do well*, not that they should literally break a leg. If it's raining cats and dogs, it means the rain is pouring down hard, not that cats and dogs are dropping from the sky.

Individual words and idiomatic phrases can act as identifying flags for our characters. I had a friend once who would always exclaim, "Fantastic!" whenever anything went wrong. She didn't mean it was great that things went wrong. For her, the word "fantastic" became her signature word used in place of an expletive. It was her personal idiom.

Take the word "yes," for example. There are many ways to say "yes." Here are a few:

Yeppers
Yeah
Yep
Sure
Whatever
Surely
You're right
Spot on
A splendid idea
Let's do it

Right on

You got it

Amen, brother

Hallelujah

Using an idiomatic word or phrase in conjunction with a particular character gives the reader an easy-to-spot reference as to who this person is. The character becomes instantly recognizable to the reader. Evelyn Cole, a friend and a great writer (www.evelyn-cole.com), calls this a "Howdie." It's as though the character is standing up and waving at the reader, saying, "Howdie, it's me!" Whenever one of her characters uses a verbal 'Howdie,' the reader doesn't need a dialogue tag to know who's speaking.

Of course, we can't overdo our "howdies." Not all characters can use an idiomatic word or phrase as an identifying characteristic, or the novel will bog down in the land of "cutsie." And readers will put the story away unfinished. But carefully selecting a specific idiom or two to use with one or two particular characters can add the depth and the distinctive voice you need to make those characters unique.

Exercise #4: Idioms Make It Real*

(To explore idioms for character use)

SET YOUR TIMER FOR 20 MINUTES and make the following lists:

Write out at least 8-10 ways to say, "Maybe."

Then write another list of 8-10 ways to say, "No."

Make another list of 8-10 ways to say, "I'm not sure."

Then try other idioms, such as: Let's go; Stop; Do it; Come here; Go away; Buy it; Drive; I hate you; I love you.

After you compiled your lists, consider what type of person would use each one. What idioms from each list work for each particular type of person (ex: a cowboy, an introvert, an aggressive woman, etc.)? If you combine the lists according to type of user and define the user type at the top of each sheet, you will have a ready-made listing of idioms for your characters to use that will help add authenticity to their speech.

Give yourself **20 MINUTES** to complete making your lists of how to say different words/phrases, then compile your lists and save them for use with your characters either now or in the future.

Lesson #5: My, Aren't We Different?

WE HAVE BEEN TALKING so far about characters whose ethnic origins and/or educational backgrounds are totally dissimilar. But sometimes our characters are fairly similar. They could be siblings, or even identical twins. Or close childhood friends who went to the same schools, or cousins with similar familial backgrounds. They grew up in the same socio-economic bracket and had the same type of education and religious training. Characters who are pretty much the same.

How do we write these characters' dialogue and have each one stand out, distinct from the other? By using the same techniques we have been using all along. Only now the differences between the characters will be more subtle, the discrepancies in how they express themselves more narrow in scope.

The best way I've found to approach this is to concentrate on **who they are as people**. Their personal differences in the way they look at life, the things they believe in, the ideas they trust, their philosophy of life, all will separate them as individuals.

For example, I once met a set of identical twins. They looked exactly alike, they dressed alike, and their voices even sounded alike. And yet, no one mixed them up once they started talking because their personalities shone through their words. One was quieter and more analytical than the other. One was excitable, the other a bit calmer. One trusted everyone she met, the other was reserved until she got to know you. One loved to gossip, the other held secrets close. One was an outgoing, optimistic soul, the other more cautious about the dangers abroad in the world. Two identical young women who grew up in the same house and went to the same schools, but they had two totally different personalities. And the way they spoke, the words they chose and how they combined them, set them apart from each other.

When we know exactly who our characters are (see *Workbook #1: Character, Setting, Story*), and what the basic makeup of their personality is, we can then put the appropriate words in their mouths in such a way that who they are is unmistakable to the reader.

*Exercise #5: My, Aren't We Different?**

(Purpose of Exercise: To make similar characters sound unique)

WRITE A DIALOGUE BETWEEN two characters who have similar backgrounds, ethnic origins, educational levels and careers. They can be new friends, old friends or even relatives. They have just moved to a new city and are looking for an apartment they can share. They are discussing the relative merits of the place they are now touring, a place that is outside the normal scope of what they have been looking at. (ex: They have been looking at large apartment buildings and this is a duplex. Or vice versa.)

Write your dialogue between these two characters so that each one stands out from the other. In this scene, the reader needs to "hear" the characters' personalities, their beliefs, their unique philosophy of life that makes their speech patterns easily recognizable and separate from each other.

It is easy to make characters with widely diverse backgrounds and/or ethnic origins sound unique. It is far more difficult to make people with similar backgrounds sound different from each other. The purpose here is to find what makes each character unique and integrate that into their speech patterns.

Set your timer for **20 MINUTES** and begin writing.

Lesson #6: To Tag, Or Not To Tag

A DIALOGUE TAG IS a word or words that precede, interrupt or follow a line of dialogue and that lets the reader know who is speaking. Some writers get quite creative in the use of dialogue tags. But this is truly an instance where less is most definitely more.

There are two types of dialogue tags: Precise, and what I call Invisible.

Precise dialogue tags tell the reader **how** the dialogue is being said. They make the reader concentrate on the how of the dialogue instead of the what. For writers new to the craft that might not seem like a big deal. But consider this: The purpose of dialogue is to **impart information**. If readers concentrate on the tone of voice, then they are not paying enough attention to the information being imparted.

Invisible dialogue tags fade into the background. They allow the dialogue to stand on its own merit. For myself, I find this rule of thumb works best: If the dialogue needs a modifier to let the reader know how it's being said, it's not effective dialogue and needs to be reworked. In other words, if a character's tone of voice is scathing, or haughty, or angry or loving, the words the character says should clearly reflect that emotion. If it doesn't, not even a precise dialogue tag will fix it. It needs to be redone.

The very best dialogue tag is "said." Don't be fooled by this little word, or by the exhortation not to repeat words too often in your text. "Said" performs a type of miracle every time you use it. It virtually vanishes before the reader's eyes. The brain picks up the name of the person speaking and skims right over the word "said." And to a large extent, "asked," "answered" and "replied" work the same way.

But writers new to the craft of fiction (and creative nonfiction), and even some experienced writers who should know better, love to get creative with dialogue tags. They'll throw in such terms as: he snarled, moaned, snapped, hissed, whimpered, groaned, whined, shouted, sneered, growled, and on and on, thinking that it makes their dialogue even better. (For a wonderful list of creative Precise Dialogue Tags, visit my writer friend Sharyl Heber's website. They're all actual dialogue tag words she's found in her reading: www.saheber.blogspot.com and click on the Said Replacements page at the right.)

But Precise Dialogue Tags **don't** make dialogue better. When readers come across such imaginative writing as:

1. "I thought I'd find you here," *he ambushed;*
2. "You are such a jerk," *she belittled;* or
3. "This will never work, not for you," *he jinxed,*

two things happen. First, their eye stops on the tag word because it's standing there yelling, "Notice me! Notice me!" which pulls readers out of the story for a moment. If there are a lot of those creative tags, they add up to a lot of moments, which in the end destroys the full enjoyment of the story.

The second thing that happens is that readers start thinking about **how** the words are being said instead of paying attention to **what** the character is saying, and why he or she is using those specific words. And if the tag is amazingly inappropriate, such as *'he piloted'* or *'she meowed,'* or *'he torpedoed'* (yes, all actual tags used in pieces of published writing), the reader might simply laugh at the writing, the image portrayed—and the writer. Again, that destroys the enjoyment of the story, and the credibility of the writer.

Another word of caution: **Don't use "said" in conjunction with adverbs.** Adverbs are telling words. They tell readers how instead of showing them what. They have little or no place anywhere in your writing. Ever. Making a Precise Dialogue Tag by using an adverb with "said," as in: *he said scathingly; she said demurely*, is, at best, lazy writing. It's making the tag do the work instead of letting the dialogue carry its own weight. The right words put in the right order will show the scathing or demure tone of voice. At worst, these kinds of Precise Dialogue Tags are clunky and pull the reader out of the story. And that leads to the reader putting the book down, unfinished.

The best way around Precise Dialogue Tags is to substitute inner thoughts and/or bits of action to attribute specific lines of dialogue to individual characters. This also allows you to show motivation and drop clues to future events.

So here's the rule: Hone your dialogue so it expresses what needs to be expressed, use bits of action and inner thoughts to attribute dialogue, and, when needed, use the miraculous Invisible Tag, "said."

Exercise #6: To Tag, Or Not To Tag*

(Purpose of Exercise: To find alternatives to Precise Dialogue Tags)

THIS THREE-PART EXERCISE SHOULD take less than an hour to complete.

Part A) Write a scene between two people who are meeting for the first time. It can be at work, church, school or a social occasion. Be sure to build in conflict of some sort so the scene is interesting to the reader and has a point of some kind.

As part of this scene, use **only Precise Dialogue Tags**, that is words that denote speaking combined with adverbs: i.e., "Yeah, right," he uttered disdainfully.

You can use bits of action in the scene, and internal dialogue, but keep both to a minimum. Concentrate on tagging the dialogue with words that show **how** the words are being spoken.

Set your timer for **15 MINUTES** and start writing.

Part B) Now rewrite the scene, **eliminating all the Precise Dialogue Tags** but still imparting the same information to the reader. Consider whether the dialogue itself needs to change to relay the information, and if it conveys the emotion of the speaker. Then look to see whether bits of action can be used to enhance the information imparted, or if adverbial phrases work best.

Concentrate on keeping the same feel to the scene; i.e., if the characters are antagonistic in the original version, don't let them be nice to each other in the second. Keep the tension high and stick to the original purpose of the scene. (Ex: Purpose of scene: To let the boss's nephew know in polite terms, "You might be the boss's new wunderkind, but I rule the roost around here.")

Set your timer for **15 MINUTES** for this rewrite and write until the timer dings.

Part C) Now read each of these scenes aloud, either to someone or to yourself. (You should always read your dialogue out loud, even if only to yourself. Your ear will pick up discrepancies your eye misses.) As you read, listen carefully. Then answer the following questions:

1. In each version, are you more aware of **how** the characters are speaking, or **what** they are saying?

2. Do Precise Dialogue Tags help or interfere with the flow of the scene?

3. Which version is more interesting to listen to?

4. Does the elimination of Precise Dialogue Tags and the use of action bits and inner thoughts in the second scene help the scene feel fuller and more satisfying?

5. Does the use of action bits and inner thoughts add clues and motivations to the second scene that are missing in the Precise Tags scene?

Take about **10 MINUTES** to finish this part of the exercise.

Lesson #7: Indirect Directness

SOMETIMES YOU RUN INTO a situation where you need to impart a specific piece of information, but can't figure how to do it without writing a long, boring scene that really has little to do with the story. The crucial nugget of information is contained within the scene, but the rest of the scene is extraneous to the plot.

The information can be something someone says, something someone sees, something a character infers, or merely an atmosphere the reader needs to know about to understand what was lost, or what a character stands to gain. To have one character simply tell this one tiny nugget of information to another character would feel forced and destroy the pace of the story. But so would delineating the entire boring scene of, say, a dinner party, a school play, a church service, a courtroom trial or an argument where only one line of dialogue is crucial to the story plot.

So how do writers solve this dilemma? By using a technique I call **Indirect Directness**. This technique summarizes the entire scene, dialogue and all, into one or two short paragraphs, inserting the one critical line of dialogue into the summary. And if the purpose is to create an atmosphere or reveal an attitude or judgment, you might not need to use any actual dialogue in the paragraph(s), only the summary of what was said.

Summarizing dialogue allows writers to:

1. **control the pace** of a scene,
2. **boil dialogue down** to its essence and emphasize the most important part, line or lines,
3. **drop clues** to future events,
4. **reveal important attitudes** of the characters,
5. **make inferences** and/or judgments
6. **avoid sentimentality**.

Using Indirect Directness, the writer can describe the tones of voices without resorting to dialogue that is tedious or boring, and shape the scene so that it becomes an integral part of moving the plot forward instead of a plodding scene that slows things down.

Indirect Directness (Summarized Dialogue) is **not a license to indulge in reams of narrative**. It's purpose is to boil down the essence of the extraneous scene into **as few words as possible**: one, two or three **short** paragraphs **at most**. By boiling the scene down this way, you will give the one line of dialogue, the atmosphere created by the summary or the judgment made by the POV character, prime place of attention for the reader. It's the fastest way to get across valuable information that can't be done any other way except by a long, boring scene that digresses from the plot.

Using Indirect Directness lets readers get the flavor of the scene without having to suffer through a blow-by-blow rendition of extraneous dialogue. It keeps readers interested and gives them the information they need quickly. And it pushes them to read on, and what author doesn't want that?

*Exercise #7: Indirect Directness**
(To impart important information without writing a boring scene)

SET UP A SITUATION in which one character is going on and on about something. It could be complaining about grades, carping about a coworker, arguing with a spouse about the children, or recounting an accident to a friend. Use narrative summary to craft this scene, interjecting only those lines of dialogue that are necessary to the story—if there are any. Such dialogue could be a short exchange between the characters, the listener's occasional response, or the speaker's main point. Be sure to intersperse the narrative with appropriate stage bits and scene setting as needed.

Example from: *Sins of the Past*, by Susan Tuttle, chapter 3

This example gives a portrait of what Sabrina's life had been like before the tragedy, the kind of neighborhood she lived in, and shows how hard Anne is working to make things "normal" for Sabrina. This could have been a long, tedious scene, complete with inane dialogue that bored the reader. Instead, Indirect Directness boiled it down to a single paragraph that shows what Sabrina's life was like before tragedy struck, and gives a clue to why she is so devastated by the loss of that life. Anne's line of dialogue, "Just imagine," points out the discrepancy between Anne's innocent, normal imaginings and Sabrina's inability to imagine anything but the sight of her dead husband.

It was an old-fashioned dinner, chicken fricassee, one of Anne's specialties, with homemade biscuits, peas, a cabbage salad and a Jell-O mold. Sabrina pushed her food around on her plate while Anne and Donald caught her up on the latest news of the neighborhood. The Walkers had moved, the new people would be coming in sometime in the next week, a mixed-racial couple with three children, very nice, Anne had met them two days ago when they had been painting in the house. Joe Masterson had finally gotten his promotion; they were in Hawaii, celebrating. The Devlins built an addition, a family room with an indoor hot tub. "Just imagine," Anne said. Claire Thomas' little girl had fallen out of a tree in the park and broken her arm, and Anne and Donald's own daughter, Donna, was pregnant, due in six months, their first grandchild. Sabrina listened, smiled, nodded, but said very little. She absorbed in silence the comforting warmth of her friends, amazed that her tragedy had so little impact on the normal course of life around her.

Now set your timer for **15 MINUTES** and begin writing your Indirect Directness scene.

Lesson #8: Subliminal Clues From Subtext

PEOPLE DON'T ALWAYS SAY what they mean. In fact, most of the time what they say on the surface and what they feel inside are two different things.

This discrepancy between what we feel and the veneer of social manners affects the way we express ourselves. Think about it. If you are angry with someone for whatever reason, but are out in public and need to convey information about, say, a party that will take place over the weekend and don't want to make a scene, the words you choose will be sightly (or greatly) different—and delivered in a different tone—than those you would choose if you were on good terms with that person.

Or consider this scenario: You are having lunch with a close friend who is complaining about her husband and needs your support. She does not know you are sleeping with the man and you can't let her know or it would ruin your friendship. That secret knowledge will color everything you say, and how you say it.

Or perhaps your sister needs to go to the bank on her lunch hour, but you know your boyfriend is going to rob that branch at that time. You don't want her to get hurt, but you can't tell her about Kurt's plans because you know she will call the police. What you say in trying to talk her out of her visit to the bank will be driven by your great need to ensure her safety while keeping your secret.

Or you go on a job interview. The position requires experience and skills just a bit out of your range, but you need (or desperately want) this particular job. You have to shine to your perspective boss without letting him know the limits of your skills. Your subconscious subtext will direct how you phrase your words to make yourself desirable to his company.

This **underlying need** is called **subtext**, the text that goes on under what is visible on the surface. It's the inner wants and desires that drive people to do what they do, and it affects both their words and actions. A man on a date with the intention of sleeping with the woman will phrase his responses to her differently than if he was merely escorting a friend's friend in whom he has no romantic interest. Most of the time subtext is unconscious; it's our subconscious' way of getting what it wants without giving away its motives. But sometimes the speaker is well aware of the subtext seething below the surface of his/her words. And, although it's more rare, sometimes it's the hearer who is aware of the speaker's hidden subtext.

As writers, considering the subtext that goes on below the surface of our characters' verbal speech helps us add richness and depth to their words. It also helps increase the suspense and/or tension in the scene and draws the reader even further into the story.

Whenever you have dialogue that doesn't sound quite right, but you can't figure out why, check to make sure you have considered the subtext—the hidden motives—beneath what the character is saying to make sure you have chosen exactly the right words in the right order. Sometimes all inadequate dialogue needs is to be run through the subtext mill.

*Exercise #8: Subliminal Clues From Subtext**

(Purpose of Exercise: To learn to consider subtext
when crafting dialogue)

WRITE A SCENE BETWEEN two people who are talking about where their relationship is going. You can set the scene at any time you like: past, present or future. You can disguise their inner desire—to figure out where they go from here—with an immediate situation: ie, after the war, they need to decide if they will stay in the ruined city or travel somewhere else. Or you can have them actually discussing the subject of their future.

Neither character wants to hurt the other and neither wants to break up. But neither wants what the other is suggesting, and they don't know how to express directly what they are feeling without hurting the other person. And each is determined not to do that.

In this scene, each character's inner agenda for the future of their relationship needs to be different (ex: one wants marriage, kids and a white picket fence; the other wants to co-habitate, no kids, no true commitment). You can make this a full scene, with action bits and internal dialogue, but focus mainly on what the two characters want to say to each other and how the subtext of what they are feeling and unable (or unwilling) to express colors what they actually say to each other.

When you finish this scene, go back and make sure that the subtext (ie, the inner desire) of each character's dialogue is the driving force of what each says aloud. If it's not, change the outer dialogue until it is directed and affected by the inner motivations of the character.

Set your timer for **20 MINUTES** and begin now.

Examples From My Class Writing

THESE ARE EXAMPLES OF WRITINGS I do in my workshops along with my students as I teach each lesson. Please bear in mind that they are done in the 15-20 minute sessions and have not been edited or corrected.

Lesson #1: Talking Heads
Dialogue Only

"Aren't you ready yet?"

"I don't think I want to go."

"What do you mean, not go? We have to go. It's your sister's wedding, for chrisakes."

"I-I'm not feeling very well today."

"That's convenient."

"What is that supposed to mean?"

"Forget it."

"No, I won't forget it. What do you mean?"

"It's just that your rivalry with Edna gets out of hand at times, that's all."

"Rivalry? What are you talking about?"

"Neither one of you can stand the other getting something the other doesn't have."

"You're crazy. I'm thrilled Edna's getting married."

"Only because you already are. Don't you remember what she did at our wedding?"

"So she fainted. It was hot and she hadn't eaten and the stress was so high... it wasn't her fault."

"You hadn't eaten either and I didn't see you keel over. Everyone danced attendance around her all night because of it, like we weren't even there. And it was our wedding!"

"So, you want me to go and do something like that to her, is that what you mean?"

"No, what I mean is your not showing up will ruin it for her. That's why you don't want to go."

"I'm sick, you jerk. You'd rather I went and threw up all over the place?"

"You were fine at breakfast."

"Well, I'm not fine now."

"You look fine. And we're going. If you don't show up it will kill your mother, and you know it. Why do you want to hurt that wonderful woman?"

"I don't want to hurt anyone! Especially me."

"You? What does that mean?"

"Forget it."

"No, what does that mean, hurt yourself? Lydia—"

"Forget it. I'm dressed, let's go, since it's so important to you."

"Lydia, what—"

"Stop it! I don't want to talk about him — I mean it. Let's go."

"Him? Who, the groom? Jeffrey? What do you — Oh. I see."

"No, you don't see. You never see, that's half the problem. So let's just get this over with, okay?"

"No. Now I don't think I want to go. At least, not to the wedding. I'll be at the Blue Diamond. Don't follow me."

"As if!"

Full Scene

Jake leaned against the doorframe and looked at Lydia where she sat at the dressing table, coloring her lips. Her dress lay across the foot of the canopied bed, shoes on the burbur rug below. He slid his hands into his tux pants pockets and narrowed his eyes at her.

"Aren't you ready yet?" he asked.

Lydia sighed and set the lipstick in the porcelain dish on the tabletop. She shook her head.

"I don't think I want to go."

"What do you mean, not go?" Jake straightened up, took a step into the room. Lydia's eyes widened. Her heart thudded. "We have to go. It's your sister's wedding, for chrisakes."

Lydia dropped her gaze and turned on the bench, put her back to Jake. It was easier to talk to him if she didn't have to look at him. Easier not to say what she knew shouldn't say.

"I-I'm not feeling very well today," she murmured. Jake snorted.

"That's convenient."

Anger twisted in Lydian's gut. Why couldn't he ever just take her word for things? Why did he always have to read something into what was supposed to be nothing?

"What is that supposed to mean?" she asked.

Despite her resolve to remain cool and aloof, her voice rose, betraying her anger. Jake shook his head and made a dismissive gesture with his hand. He gave her a look of pure disdain.

"Forget it."

That was exactly what Lydia wanted to do, but she couldn't seem to make her mouth stop moving. Anger and fear were taking over, removing rationality from the equation. How dare he dismiss her, dismiss her feelings, like that? She turned and glared at him.

"No, I won't forget it. What do you mean, convenient?"

Jake spread his hands as though in apology, but his cold voice belied the action.

"It's just that your rivalry with Edna gets out of hand at times, that's all."

"Rivalry?" Lydia turned and fiddled with the bottles of perfume and lotion on the dressing table so she didn't have to look at Jake. "What are you talking about?"

"Neither one of you can stand the other getting something you don't have."

"You're crazy." She shoved a perfume bottle away. "I'm thrilled Edna's getting married."

"Only because you already are." Jake walked over and sat on the bed beside her dress, began fingering the jet beads on the bodice. "Don't you remember what she did at our wedding?"

"What she—" Lydia gave a halfhearted laugh and shrugged. She hadn't realized it had bothered Jake, he'd never said anything about it before. "So she fainted. It was hot and she hadn't eaten and the stress was so high… it wasn't her fault."

"You hadn't eaten either and I didn't see you keel over." Jake rose and walked over to her, started kneading her shoulders and neck. Her muscles were so tight with tension that it hurt. "Everyone danced attendance around her all night because of it, like we weren't even there. And it was our wedding!"

She shrugged off his hands and met his icy blue eyes in the mirror. She wondered if their arguments took as much out of him as they did her.

"So, you want me to go and do something like that to her, is that what you mean?"

"No, what I mean is your not showing up will ruin it for her. That's why you don't want to go."

Lydia surged off the bench and stalked to the bed.

"I'm sick, you jerk." She flung out her arms. "You'd rather I went and threw up all over the place?"

Jake crossed his arms — his intransigent stance.

"You were fine at breakfast."

"Well, I'm not fine now." She stood glaring at him, arms akimbo— her intransigent stance.

"You look fine. And we're going. If you don't show up it will kill your mother, and you know it. Why do you want to hurt that wonderful woman?"

God! Why did he always throw her mother in her face? Her vision misted red and she forgot to think before spoke.

"I don't want to hurt anyone! Especially me."

Silence engulfed them for a moment. Jake's arms uncrossed. Lydia, heart thudding, picked up the long blue gown. This couldn't be happening, she couldn't have said that. She prayed in vain that Jake hadn't heard, hadn't realized what she'd said.

"You?" Jake's voice, when he finally spoke, was quiet, speculative. "What does that mean?"

"Forget it." Lydia pulled the dress over her head and smoothed it down her body.

"No, what does that mean, hurt yourself? Lydia—"

"Forget it." She shoved her feet into the shoes. "I'm dressed, let's go, since it's so important to you."

"Lydia, what—"

"Drop it! I don't want to talk about him — I mean it." Omygod, what was she saying? Where was this coming from? "I don't want to talk about the wedding. Let's just go."

Jake grabbed her arms and stared into her eyes. Lydia felt like an open book, fear and horror mixed into a truth she couldn't acknowledge, a tale spread before Jake's questing eyes.

"Him? Who, the groom? Jeffrey? What do you —" Jake let her go with a small shove. "Oh. I see."

"No, you don't see. You never see, that's half the problem. So let's just get this over with, okay?"

She wanted to go to Jake, cling to him, but instead picked up the metallic blue wrap and threw it over her shoulders. Jake shook his head and backed away.

"No. Now I don't think I want to go. At least, not to the wedding." He stalked to the door, then turned to glower at her before he disappeared. "I'll be at the Blue Diamond. Don't follow me."

"As if!" Lydia shouted, putting all her panic and anger into the two words. Then she pulled off the wrap, dropped onto the bed and burst into tears.

Exercise #2: It's How You Say It
Speech Fragments:

(Teen, high school, valley girl) "No shit, Sherlock. Put all together it spells 'Duh.' I mean, what's your childhood trauma, anyway?"

(Black man, deep south) "I been puzzlin' on it ever since it happen. Be maybe worser 'n I ever seen, I'se swear. Mm-mmm. Ain't nobody in his right mind do that to a little girl. Not nobody."

(Self-educated snob with social pretensions) "It behooves you to consider the consequences, my dear. Your actions foretell possible problems for the future."

(Woman in late twenties, well educated, quirky way of looking at life.) "Who the hell are you? How did you get in here? And why can I see through you?" Mackenzie shook her head and buried her hands in her hair. "Damn, I knew I shouldn't have eaten that shrimp."

(Six year old girl) "Can we go now, Aunt Claire? Please? Can I ride the Ferris Wheel on my own? I'll be good, promise. I won't tease Joey, or talk too much, or even scream. I promise. Please? Please, please, please?"

Exercise #3: Writing for Your Audience

Anglo-Saxon Words

It wouldn't have happened if Bennie had read the schedule right. Or actually listened to the <u>woman</u> who gushed with <u>happiness</u> about the session. It was a <u>tale</u> he'd tell to anyone who got near him in the long <u>lonely</u> years ahead.

Children's Bank Authors and Illustrators Presentation, he thought the flyer said. Considering his <u>wretched</u> circumstances, the amount of money he needed to get the mob off his back, robbing a bank in a library wouldn't be as hard as a real bank building. And a children's bank, no less. When he overheard the <u>woman</u> say there would be three there, his heart soared. He could barely <u>hide</u> his grin. Though why <u>youthful folk</u> would need three banks, he had no idea.

He raced back to his <u>house</u> to make his preparations. He dismissed the idea of <u>help</u>. It shouldn't be hard to take money from babies, so why <u>share</u> the proceeds? He loaded his gun, tied a bandanna around his neck (so lucky that in Arizona a neckerchief was almost a uniform), and grabbed a paper sack to hold the cash. Then he set off to <u>feed</u> his money hunger.

The <u>town</u> library was full of patrons that day. Even the bank room was full of people sitting on chairs with notebooks in their hands. At the front of the room he saw a long table behind which sat six <u>women</u> <u>dressed</u> in colorful skirts and blouses. None were especially young, but one lady looked quite tiny and frail. Not a suit in sight. Which was strange. Didn't bank <u>folk</u> wear suits and ties and stuff? Maybe because this was for children they'd relaxed the rules.

He sat down and listened to the <u>woman</u> at the podium speak in <u>kingly</u> tones about the <u>books</u> that had been written, as she <u>gave</u> information about the writers. He <u>searched</u> around for the safe—or safes —but found no sign of one. He shivered. Despite the bright <u>sunlight</u>, the room felt <u>cold</u>.

Finally he could stand it no longer. Time to <u>begin</u> the show. He <u>rose up</u> from his seat, <u>came near</u> the front of the room, pulled his gun and shouted, "Hand over the cash or <u>die</u>!"

A <u>deep</u> silence met his words. Bennie felt strong and <u>virile</u> as the folks cowered in their seats. Then the little old lady behind the main table stood up, grabbed the stuffed otter that sat on the table in front of her, and whacked Bennie over the head. The rolls of quarters she'd stuffed inside the toy cracked his skull and by the time Bennie woke, the cops had him cuffed and ready for transport. The little old lady, emcee of the Children's Book Authors and Illustrators Presentation, looked down at him and shook her head.

"I always come prepared, young man. After all, writing can be <u>murder</u>!"

French/Latin Words

It wouldn't have happened if Bennie had read the schedule right. Or actually listened to the <u>female</u> who gushed with <u>felicity</u> about the session. It was a <u>story</u> he'd tell to anyone who got near him in the long <u>solitary</u> years ahead.

Children's Bank Authors and Illustrators Presentation, he thought the flyer said. Considering his <u>miserable</u> circumstances, the amount of money he needed to get the mob off his back, robbing a bank in a library wouldn't be as hard as a real bank building. And a children's bank, no less. When he overheard the <u>female</u> say there would be three there, his heart soared. He could barely <u>conceal</u> his grin. Though why <u>Juvenile people</u> would need three banks, he had no idea.

He raced back to his <u>domicile</u> to make his preparations. He dismissed the idea of <u>help</u>. It shouldn't be hard to take money from babies, so why <u>portion</u> the proceeds? He loaded his gun, tied a bandanna around his neck (so lucky that in Arizona a neckerchief was almost a uniform), and grabbed a paper sack to hold the cash. Then he set off the <u>nourish</u> his money hunger.

The <u>urban</u> library was full of patrons that day. Even the bank room was full of people sitting on chairs with notebooks in their hands. At the front of the room he saw a long table behind which sat six <u>females clothed</u> in colorful skirts and blouses. None were especially young, but one lady looked quite tiny and frail. Not a suit in sight. Which was strange. Didn't bank <u>people</u> wear suits and ties and stuff? Maybe because this was for children they'd relaxed the rules.

He sat down and listened to the <u>female</u> at the podium speak in <u>regal</u> tones about the <u>literature</u> that had been written, as she <u>presented</u> information about the writers. He <u>looked</u> around for the safe—or safes—but found no sign of one. He shivered. Despite the bright <u>solar activity</u>, the room felt <u>frigid</u>.

Finally he could stand it no longer. Time to <u>commence</u> the show. He <u>ascended</u> from his seat, <u>approached</u> the front of the room, pulled his gun and shouted, "Hand over the cash or <u>perish</u>!"

A <u>profound</u> silence met his words. Bennie felt strong and <u>manly</u> as the folks cowered in their seats. Then the little old lad behind the main table stood up, grabbed the stuffed otter that sat on the table in front of her, and whacked Bennie over the head. The roll of quarters she'd stuffed inside the toy cracked his skull and by the time Bennie woke, the cops had him cuffed and ready for transport. The little old lady, emcee of the Children's Book Authors and Illustrators Presentation, looked down at him and shook her head.

"I always come prepared, young man. After all, writing can be <u>homicide</u>!"

Lesson #4: Idioms Make It Real:

Yes: Of course, certainly, yeah, yo, uh-huh, sure, why not, okay, yowzer, that's a go, absolutely, I'm on board, Go for it, yep, right, okey-dokey, right on

No: Nope, nah, uh-uh, ain't gonna happen, won't fly, absolutely not, not, good night, not me, in your dreams, *nyet*, no-no nanette, never, forget it, not on your life, nada, wrong, no siree, noperoonie

I'm not sure: perhaps, probably, could be, if you say so, I'm thinking about it, haven't decided yet, maybe, we'll see, kinda

Let's go: come on, move it, get your ass in gear, hie, hurry up, don't dawdle, hop to it

Stop: halt, quit, cut it out, put an end to it, enough, avast, cease, cease and desist, *basta*

Do it: Get it in gear, stat, get it done, make it happen

Come here: approach, get nearer, on this spot now, stand before me

Go Away: flee, get lost, get outa here, begone, shoo, scram, skedaddle, amscray, beat it

Buy it: put in on the card, card it, purchase, acquire it, get it, make it yours, possess it, transfer ownership, fork over the cash, grease a palm, trade green for it

Drive: motor, put pedal to the metal, navigate, put it in gear, wheels up

I hate you: you turd, I abhor you, creep-o, degenerate, ass-wipe

I love you: my heart, my *amore*, you're my life, you're my *raison d'etre, j'tadore, mi corazon*

Lesson #5: My, Aren't We Different?

Scenario: Two cousins who grew up a few houses from each other, are looking for an apartment in the city.

"I'm not sure this a good idea," Jennilyn said as they walked through the glass doors. "It's not what we talked about."

"Oh, come on, cuz." Ashley ran her hand down the embossed silver wallpaper that lined the foyer walls. "Live a little, girl. Take a risk. Be bold and daring."

"That's easy for you to say." Jennilyn watched as Ashely reached out and pushed the button to summon the elevator. "You've lived in places like this before."

"And it's exciting, Jen. I kid you not. You'll get to meet all sorts of people, from all walks of life. Broaden your world view, if you get my drift."

"I don't need broadening, I like myself just the way I am. And we can't afford a place like this, Ashley."

The elevator arrived. The doors opened and Jennilyn gasped. She'd never seen anything so exotic, so luxurious in her life. And this was just the elevator!

"A chandelier? There's a chandelier in the elevator? What kind of building is this, Ashley," she asked as her cousin pushed her into the mirror-lined car, "that they've got a chandelier in the elevator?"

"It's the bees knees, cuz. A place fit for the Sultan of Swat."

Ashley pushed the button for the tenth floor. The elevator doors whooshed closed on a waft of jasmine-scented air, and with a little jerk the car began moving upward. Jennilyn grabbed onto the polished brass handrail and hung on as though they were flying out into space.

The apartment door stood ajar when they reached the tenth floor and followed the arrows posted on the silver-paper-lined walls, down to the left and around the corner into a private ell. They could hear the gentle strains of classical music emanating from the apartment. The luscious scent of baking bread caressed their senses and made Jennilyn's mouth water. Ashley pushed the apartment door open, her hand beside brushed brass numbers that read 1027C, and stepped inside, towing Jennilyn behind her.

"Hello! Anyone here? Come out, come out, wherever you are!"

"God, Ashley, you sound like an idiot," Jennilyn whispered. "No one will take us seriously if you can't act like an adult.:

"Oh, give it a rest, cuz. Hey, we've got money in hand, here," she called out. "You renting this place, or what?"

Silence answered her. Ashley looked at Jennilyn and shrugged, then grabbed her hand and pulled her along on her self-tour of the apartment.

"Oooh, it's got a side-by-side fridge, Jen! And an indoor grill. I'd say this is a par-tay kitchen for sure!"

"We don't cook, Ashley," Jennilyn said, eying all the stainless steel with a jaundiced eye.

"There's a solution for that," Ashley said, guiding Jennilyn into the living room. "We either learn or meet a guy who'll do it for us. I vote for the latter."

"Why isn't anyone here to show us this? Where's the owner?" Jennilyn asked over and over as Ashley oohed and aahed over the corner fireplace, the built-in bookshelves, the two full bathrooms, the two bedrooms with walk-in closets and the small den where she could set up her computer and music paraphernalia. The ceilings held central plaster rosettes and tasteful chandeliers, with cove moldings curing onto the walls. The only jarring note for Jennilyn was the bars on all the windows, obviously not needed this high up. They returned to the living room where Jennilyn went to the window and looked out. Ashely spun in a circle in the center of the large room.

"This is definitely way too expensive for us, Ashley," Jennilyn said.

"I don't care how much this place costs. I'm in love, Jen! String orchestra and bursting lights in love. We'll rob a bank if we have to. This is perfect for us. We have to have it!"

"No, we don't. What we have to have is what we can afford. Ashley, you need to get serious here—"

"Good afternoon, ladies."

The deep voice rolled toward them from the entryway. Jennilyn and Ashley turned to find a tall man standing just outside the kitchen doorway, staring at them with deep, fathomless eyes. Behind him, the apartment door was closed. Jennilyn's heart skipped a beat when she realized that the safety chain had been engaged. The man smiled, the menace in the movement curdling Jennilyn's blood. He held a rope in his hands.

"I'm sure you will love it here," he said in a quiet voice they had to strain to hear. "It's well sound-proofed and very private. You don't have to worry about disturbing anyone. As for the cost, all I require is your presence."

He stalked toward them and Jennilyn screamed.

Lesson #6: To Tag or Not To Tag

Scene with Precise Dialogue Tags:

Mandy arrived early for work on Monday, sure this was the day her promotion would be announced. Elaine Mallory had retired a month ago, and Mandy's application for the position was on Mr. Carson's desk almost before the door closed behind the old bag. When they'd left last night, he'd said he would have a surprise for everyone in the morning. And he'd winked at her.

Mandy hummed her favorite song, *Respect,* as she rode up in the elevator, practicing in her mind how she would react to the announcement: please, surprised and humble, with just a soupcon of self-aggrandizing congratulations. That should hit just the right note.

Her first surprise were the lights, which were on in an office suite that should have been deserted. Had someone broken in? Mandy's heart began to thud as she inched her way across the reception area toward what she thought of as her new office. The lights were on in there, too, and she could see a shadow moving behind the glass panel in the not-quite-shut door.

She pushed on the door. It swung open on silent hinges. A woman stood to her left, holding a picture frame and staring at the wall. Mandy took a deep breath and put on her upper-management persona.

"Who are you?" she demanded imperiously.

The woman spun around with a gasp. She clutched the frame to her chest as though it were a shield.

"Oh, my goodness!" she exclaimed breathily. "You scared me!"

"I said, who are you?" Mandy repeated authoritatively, giving the woman a searing glare. "What are you doing here?"

The woman smiled and stuck out her hand.

"I'm Jenny Ayres, the new Marketing Director," she said genially. "I was so excited I couldn't sleep, so I thought I'd get a jump on the moving-in process."

"You're who? What?" Mandy said confusedly. Her head whirled. This couldn't be happening!

"Didn't Jack tell you?" Jenny queried puzzledly.

"No," Mandy said stiffly. "He only said he had a surprise for us."

"Well," Jenny cooed confidingly, "I guess that's me." She gave Mandy a huge smile and gestured to the room's guest chair. "Won't you sit for a minute so we can get acquainted? What do you do here?"

I'm the new Marketing Director, Mandy wanted to shout. But she kept her lips shut as she sat and watched Jenny Ayres — tall, thin, young, energetic Jenny Ayres — walk around the desk to perch in the swivel chair. She picked up a pen and opened a notebook.

"Let's start with your name," Jenny demanded. Obviously, there was steel beneath that lovely-looking exterior.

"Amanda Wilton," Mandy said repressively. She wasn't about to tell this bitch that everyone called her Mandy. If this Jenny was any good at her job, she'd figure it out for herself.

"And you do...? Jenny enquired curiously.

"Ad copy for our biggest clients," Mandy muttered reluctantly. "Though for the past month I've been the acting Director," she added boastingly.

"I see," Jenny said acerbically. She frowned at the schedule Mandy had finished just yesterday. "We'll need to make some changes, obviously."

Scene with Invisible Tags:

Mandy arrived early for work on Monday, sure this was the day her promotion would be announced. Elaine Mallory had retired a month ago, and Mandy's application for the position was on Mr. Carson's desk almost before the door closed behind the old bag. When they'd left last night, he'd said he would have a surprise for everyone in the morning. And he'd winked at her.

Mandy hummed her favorite song, *Respect*, as she rode up in the elevator, practicing in her mind how she would react to the announcement: please, surprised and humble, with just a soupcon of self-aggrandizing congratulations. That should hit just the right note.

Her first surprise were the lights, which were on in an office suite that should have been deserted. Had someone broken in? Mandy's heart began to thud as she inched her way across the reception area toward what she thought of as her new office. The lights were on in there, too, and she could see a shadow moving behind the glass panel in the not-quite-shut door.

She pushed on the door. It swung open on silent hinges. A woman stood to her left, holding a picture frame and staring at the wall. Mandy took a deep breath and put on her upper-management persona.

"Who are you?" Mandy's imperious tone rang in the small space. She was glad her voice didn't shake the way her body did.

The woman spun around with a gasp. She clutched the frame to her chest as though it were a shield.

"Oh, my goodness!" The woman's sweet, breathy tone made Mandy grit her teeth. "You scared me!"

"I said, who are you?" Mandy gave the woman a searing glare, tilting her head back to look down her nose at the mass of red curls, the bright blue eyes, the obvious designer outfit. "What are you doing here?"

The woman smiled and stuck out her hand. Mandy was sure she meant it to be friendly, but with suspicion growing in her heart, Mandy was in no mood to be amicable with this little twerp.

"I'm Jenny Ayres, the new Marketing Director. I was so excited I couldn't sleep, so I thought I'd get a jump on the moving-in process." The woman uttered a small laugh and shook her head. Her curls bounced and settled back into place; Mandy had to resist lifting her hand to her own hair that was cut at a discount outlet and never behaved.

"You're *who*?" Mandy asked, praying that she had heard wrong. What about her promotion? "You're what?" Her head whirled. This couldn't be happening! Mr. Carson had winked at her, for heaven's sake!

"Didn't Jack tell you?" Jenny Ayres studied her. Mandy could see confusion in her face, confusion that quickly gave way to speculation and understanding. She wondered what her own face reflected.

"No." Mandy felt so betrayed she could barely move her lips. *Jack? She calls Mr. Carson, Jack?* "He only said he had a surprise for us."

"Well, I guess that's me." Jenny's tone and smile were still friendly, but Mandy could now sense calculation behind both. Jenny gestured to the room's guest chair. "Won't you sit for a minute so we can get acquainted? What do you do here?"

I'm the new Marketing Director, Mandy wanted to shout. But she kept her lips shut as she sat and watched Jenny Ayres — tall, thin, young, energetic Jenny Ayres — walk around the desk to perch in the swivel chair. The Marketing Director picked up a pen and opened a notebook.

"Let's start with your name, then." Jenny's steady gaze and her tone demanded an answer. Obviously, there was steel beneath that lovely-looking exterior.

Mandy decided she'd play the game, but she'd give it lip service only. No need to help out the enemy, was there? So she answered, her voice as clipped as her words.

"Amanda Wilton." No one called her Amanda, not even her parents, but she wasn't about to tell this bitch that everyone called her Mandy. If this Jenny was any good at her job, she'd figure it out for herself.

"And you do…?"

"Ad copy for our biggest clients." Mandy knew she'd given as much information as she needed to, but she couldn't help adding, with a tinge of pride in her voice that made her wince, "Though for the past month I've been the Acting Director."

"I see." Jenny's tone had become as clipped as Mandy's. She gave Mandy an enigmatic look, then frowned at the schedule Mandy had finished just yesterday. "Well, we'll need to make some changes, obviously."

Exercise #7: Indirect Directness

We crouched in the corner where the rebels had put us, afraid to so much as breathe. They'd left the woman behind to guard us, a duty which she appeared to take seriously since she kept her machine gun pointed into the center of our huddle. I estimated about two hours had passed in relative silence — once Martha had stopped sniveling — when the guard's eyes began to glaze over. But I was too worried that just the twist of my arm, so I could read my watch to check on my accuracy, would remind her we were still there so I didn't move. What did it matter, anyway? A day, an hour, a minute—when you're shoved into a corner and stood over with a gun even a second is too long.

She crossed to the window and stood at the edge, peering out with exaggerated caution. I hoped a sniper would get her right between the eyes, not that it would do us much good since the other eight rebels still held the building. She began to talk, not even glancing at us, as though she spoke to herself alone. She said her name was Lillia. Her mother had died in childbirth when Lillia was only two, her father when she was five, both shot by government forces. The rebel unit cared for her. She told us about growing up in the camp, always on the run. It was a game at first, running and hiding, filled with fear and excitement. She'd been weaned on that, the fear and excitement; it was like a drug she couldn't do without anymore. Life got boring fast, and what was the point of life if it wasn't fun and exhilarating? *Yeah*, I thought, *this is real fun for all of us, sitting here waiting to be executed so you can bring some excitement into your life*. I personally could do without it. I like boring, myself. You can count on it, trust it. Unless you live in Durangia.

Lillia wandered back over and studied us as she lit a cigarette, her gun cradled in the crook of her arm. I suppose you've all got houses, and families, she said, gardens and furniture and take walks in the park and go to movies. She'd never had furniture, or a house, never been to a movie, but she did go to the park once. At night, when it was relatively safe. Swings are fun in the dark. Then she looked straight at me.

"If things were different," she said in an astonishing plaintive tone, "would you take me to the park? In the daytime? So I could swing in the sunshine?"

I nodded. What else could I do since she'd cocked the gun and pointed it at me? Then she smiled and said I was a smart man. Too bad I would have to die this day.

Exercise #8: Subliminal Clues from Subtext

Situation: After an apocalyptic war with bloodthirsty rebels

Man (Rolle): Scarred by the loss of his wife and lover, he does not want any romantic entanglements even though he needs to partner with someone to survive.

Woman (Joceira): Hardened by the war and the killing, fiercely independent, she craves love and a caring mate.

"Do you think we should stay together?" she asked, her gaze on the smoking ruins below. Rolle knew they were far enough from the fumes to be safe, but still he watched the air currents, the way the clouds raced across the sky. If the wind shifted, they'd need to move fast.

"Why would we split up?" He looked at Joceira and suppressed a shudder at the sight of the toxic bloom on her left cheek. "That what you want?"

"No. I just thought…" She stood up and walked to the edge of the grove, leaned against a twisted trunk. Sunlight broke through the leaves and studded her like a disco ball.

"Thought what?" He wanted to get up and go to her, knew that was what she wanted. But thoughts of Carley and Rachel interfered, glued his ass to the rock as strongly as epoxy.

"Maybe you've gotten sick of me by now." Her voice was so low he had to strain to hear. "Maybe you want to move faster, not have to share your food and water, and stuff."

Was she crying? Every time he'd thought so in the past, every time her voice trembled like it did now, her face was always dry, her eyes bright and clear.

"We've been over this before," he said, unable to keep the weary frustration from his tone. "We're a team, now. You and me against the world, babe," he added, hoping to make her laugh.

He hadn't heard her laugh in a long time. She didn't now. She didn't even turn around. Rolle got up from the rock, took a step toward her.

"I'm not sick of you, Joceira. And I don't mind sharing food and water. What are friends for, anyway?"

She turned then, and damn if her face wasn't wet this time. For some reason, it rocked Rolle to his soul. Joceira had always been so steady, so single-minded through the struggle, the fighting, the death. She hadn't cried when Oscar died, or Phillip. She'd dug Rachel's grave with a set face and anger-driven hands. She'd killed her share of rads without losing a second of sleep. What the hell was she crying about when they'd finally won, when life, though still hard, could at least be rebuilt and lived with a soupcon of safety and hope?

Joceira scrubbed her face with her hands. She gave him a brilliant smile, then stuck out her hand, took his and and shook it.

"Friends. A team. Yes, that sounds good," she said, though her brittle tone didn't match her words. "What else would friends be for, Rolle? What else?"

Afterword

"Always grab the reader by the throat in the first paragraph, sink your thumbs into his windpipe in the second, and hold him against the wall until the tag line."

~Paul O'Neil

BEING A WRITER IS a fascinating occupation. By its very nature it forces us to dig deeply into our inner core, face those things that frighten us, are painful or perhaps even disgust us. And then we bring those things into the light of day—on a piece of paper, whether physical or virtual—and transform them into a story that entertains, teaches and/or enlightens whoever reads it. It helps make the world a better place.

The amount of skill needed to do all that successfully is known fully only to those engaged in the practice itself. Readers come in two main groups: those who cannot conceive of what it takes to write a story, much less an entire book; and those who think it's easy to sit down and pound out a story or even a book in a few days or weeks. But only the brave actually attempt it.

Everything we learn to increase our writing skills helps improve us human beings. We learn how to see, to hear, to contemplate and to understand in ways that most others never do. We learn to find the weaknesses in our heroes and how to use that to strengthen their characters. And, in a way, we are also strengthened. We search for the good in our villains and use that to make them human and comprehensible. And in facing our own dark side, we understand more about ourselves and those around us.

In this *Workbook #3*, you have explored two of the essential skills you need to craft compelling, unforgettable stories through plot and dialogue, whether they are pure fiction or arise from your own life as memoirs. But you need much more than these three areas of expertise before you find your strength as a writer. The other workbooks in the *Write It Right* series will give you exactly what you need to become the best writer you can possibly be, with exercises that can be used over and over again as your skills continue to grow and develop.

Workbook #1 (if you haven't yet acquired it) consists of the first three units of the *Write It Right* series: *Character, Setting* and *Story*. These are the first three essential elements of story telling, the foundation blocks, so to speak, for without compelling characters in unforgettable settings acting out amazing stories, there is nothing to write about.

Workbook #2: Point of View (POV) will take you through the murky waters of point of view. In its 15 lessons and exercises you will learn about straight, emotional and classic POV types, and the advantages and disadvantages of each one. You will then experience their variations and understand when to use which POV type to best advantage in your story telling.

Workbook #4: Scenes, Style/Voice contains lessons and exercises that will help you understand the 9 different types of scene structures and how each affects the rhythm and pacing of your stories. The Unit on

Style/Voice will help you develop your own unique writing style, a clear, consistent voice that will stand out among all the others and be readily recognizable as yours alone.

Workbook #5: Conflict/Tension, Subplot will show you how to create and sustain the tension that keeps readers turning pages through 9 tension-filled exercises. The strategies contained in the unit on Subplot will help you add depth and dimension to your work by weaving fascinating subplots into your main stories. In this workbook, you will also learn the secret to creating an effective and compelling series that satisfies readers as it pulls them through one volume to the next.

Workbook #6: Beginnings, Endings gives you 8 different formats each for opening your story and for ending your story. In Brilliant Beginnings you will also learn how to polish that all-important first sentence/first paragraph/first page so that readers are compelled to continue reading. And in Extraordinary Endings, you will learn the secrets to choosing the proper ending for whatever story you write, so that readers smile and say, "I'm so glad I read that!"

Look for the entire *Write It Right: Exercises to Unlock the Writer in Everyone* workbook series on Amazon.com in print format. Each individual unit is also available in digital format in the Kindle store, but the workbooks themselves are available only in print because I feel that is the most useful format for serious writers. You can have the book open on your desk as you work on the exercises either by hand of on the computer, and not have to keep switching from one window to another to check on the exercise parameters or re-read the lesson as you work.

Thank you for purchasing this Workbook. I hope you find it helpful on your writing journey. If you do, please take the time to write a review on Amazon.com, since that's where most of my sales come from.

In this digital age of social media, it's reader reviews that best help sell books. As does word of mouth, so be sure to tell all your writer friends about the *Write It Right* series, so they can also benefit from the program.

Also, if you'd like, please drop by my website (www.SusanTuttleWrites.com) and leave a comment or two about the photos and story/character/setting ideas you'll find (Category: Woman of 1,000 Words), the weekly writing prompts that post every Wednesday (Category: Write Over The Hump), about the *Write It Right* program, or any other writing subject that comes to mind. Or email me at aim2write@yahoo.com. I'd love to hear from you.

Susan's Books

I NEVER THOUGHT, WHEN I started to write my own stories, that one day I would produce an entire series of workbooks on how to write fiction (and creative nonfiction, because these days that genre needs to be structured in the same manner as fiction). I never thought it even when I started teaching fiction writing. Getting my novels out was my main goal. But life has a way of guiding you down paths you don't even know are there, and this is where I've been led.

What follows is a listing of the books I have out in either print or ebook format, or both—and those in process of being readied for print/e-format. The *Write It Right Workbooks* head the list, but I'm also adding in my fiction titles at the end (suspense and paranormal suspense) in case you might like to take a peek at them, too (all available on Amazon.com and Amazon Kindle). I think they're pretty great, but then, as the author, I'll admit I'm a bit prejudiced.

My hope is that my *Write It Right Workbooks* will help unlock the talent and amazing stories that reside in each and every one of you. Happy writing!

Susan's Nonfiction Books

Write It Right Workbooks available from Amazon Print:
  Workbook #1: Units 1, 2, 3: Character, Setting, Story
  Workbook #2: Unit 4: POV,
  Workbook #3: Units 5, 6: Plot, Dialogue
  Workbook #4: Units 7, 8: Scenes, Style/Voice, Conflict
  Workbook #5: Units 9, 10: Conflict/Tension, Subplot*
  Workbook #6: Units 11, 12: Beginnings, Endings*

Write It Right Individual Units available from Amazon Kindle:
  Volume 1: Character
  Volume 2: Setting
  Volume 3: Story
  Volume 4: Point of View (POV)
  Volume 5: Plot*
  Volume 6: Dialogue*
  Volume 7: Scenes*
  Volume 8: Style and Voice*
  Volume 9: Conflict/Tension*
  Volume 10: Subplot*
  Volume 11: Brilliant Beginnings*
  Volume 12: Extraordinary Endings*

*Coming soon

Susan's Fiction Books

Suspense
Tangled Webs
Sins of the Past

Paranormal Suspense
Proof of Identity

Coming Soon:
Obsession, suspense
Piece By Piece, suspense
A Matter of Identity, historical suspense
Stealing Shyon, an adult fantasy
The Skylark Series: paranormal detectives
   The Somewhen Murder
   Dead Ringer
   Someone Else's Eyes
   Tattoed in Death
Destany's Daughter, Volume I of a paranormal YA/Adult fantasy quadrilogy
It Takes Class: On the Short Side, free writes from my writing classes

www.ingramcontent.com/pod-product-compliance
Lightning Source LLC
Chambersburg PA
CBHW080543180626
46818CB00008B/3111